BY JEAN LEE LATHAM

Carry On,

MR. BOWDITCH

HOUGHTON MIFFLIN COMPANY BOSTON

Illustrated by John O'Hara Cosgrave, II

Library of Congress Catalog Card Number 55-5219
ISBN 0-395-06881-9
ISBN 0-395-13713-6(pbk.)

Printed in the United States of America

VB   50 49 48 47 46 45 44 43

CONTENTS

CHAPTER 1

THE GOOD-LUCK SPELL

Nat lay very still in the dark, trying to stay awake until his big brother, Hab, went to sleep. Nat wasn't quite sure, but he thought a good-luck spell worked better if you kept it secret. He stared out the window and watched the April breeze chase clouds across the stars. His eyelids sagged. That wouldn't do! He must stay awake to work his spell. His family needed good luck.

Why did they have so much bad luck? Was it because Father had lost his ship? Or was it because of the war? Ever since Nat could remember, the war had been going on. How long had it been? He counted back on his fingers to 1775. Four years since the war started.

His eyelids sagged again. He squinched them shut and opened them. Was Hab asleep now? Nat whispered, "Hab?"

Hab stirred and muttered, "Why don't you go to sleep?"

"I got to thinking about Salem."

Hab snorted. "You can't remember Salem. It's been four years since we moved away. Go to sleep."

Nat rubbed his eyes and stared out the window again. Four years since everything happened — since the war began, and Father lost his ship, and they moved away from Salem. How old was he then? He was four-from-six; he was two. He'd count up how old everybody had been; that would help him stay awake. Mary was four-from-thirteen; she was nine. Hab was four-from-eleven; he was seven. Lizza was four-from-eight; she was four. William was four-from-three; he was . . . he wasn't!

Hab sat up with a jerk. "What in the name of sense are you giggling about?"

"About William was four-from-three when we moved to Danvers."

"You and your numbers! Look, Nat! We have to get up early tomorrow! Mr. Baker'll be here before sunup to help us move back to Salem. Now settle down and go to sleep!"

Nat sat up and leaned his head on his knees. "Will you answer just one question, Hab?"

"What is it?"

"Is it the best good-luck spell in the world to jingle silver in your pocket when you see the new moon?"

"Of course. But you have to have silver to jingle."

Nat thought of the shilling he'd found. He hugged his knees and grinned.

The next thing Nat heard was Hab's voice saying,

"Wake up, sleepy-head." He opened his eyes. It was morning. His good-luck spell! He'd missed it! His stomach felt scared.

Hab was standing by the bed, his dark hair wet and combed, a grin like Father's on his square face. He pulled the covers off Nat. "Come on, you little towhead."

Father tramped up the steep stairs, bending his dark head where the roof slanted, and stood with his arm around Hab's shoulders, smiling down at Nat. "Hab, it's a good thing you thought of him. He's so little we might have missed him. We might just have rolled him up in the covers and never found him till we got to Salem!"

Nat laughed with them, but his stomach still felt scared. He scrambled out of bed, pulled on his trousers and shirt, and scuttled downstairs. His bowl of mush was waiting on the table. He said, "I'm not hungry."

Granny's sharp black eyes looked at him over her spectacles. "You get washed up and sit right down and eat. It isn't Christian to throw out good food, and I'm not going to carry that bowl of mush to Salem by hand."

Mother smiled and hugged Granny. "He'll eat it. Come on, dear. Let's go see how they're getting along with the loading."

Granny nodded. "We'd better. Those men will make a hurrah's nest of it."

When they had gone, Nat tried to eat, but he couldn't swallow around the lump in his throat. He carried his bowl over in the corner where little William was playing by Sammy's cradle. He'd feed his breakfast to them so it wouldn't be wasted.

Essex Street in Salem 1776

He was just scraping his bowl, and Sammy was holding up his face like a robin waiting for a worm, when Lizza came in.

"Oh, Nat! If Granny knew you didn't eat your breakfast, you'd catch it!" Lizza whispered.

Nat grinned. "But you won't tell her. You keep secrets better than anybody."

"I have to keep your secrets. Some day you'll be bigger than I am." Lizza giggled.

Nat stood by Lizza to measure. She was only eight — just two years older — but a good head taller. "You're sure I'll be bigger?"

"Of course. Some day you'll be saying, 'Lizza, bring your head over here a minute. I want something to lean my elbow on!'"

Nat stuck out his chest and put his hands in his pockets. He felt something tied up in a rag. His shilling! "Lizza, when we get to Salem, I'll tell you a real secret! The biggest secret in the world."

It was late that afternoon when Mr. Baker's wagons crossed North River into Salem and drove to Turner's Lane. Granny called, "See that big house, children? Down near the water? Your great-great-great-grandfather, Captain Turner, built that house. No other house in Salem like it. It has seven gables."

Before the wagons came to the big house with seven gables they stopped in front of a weather-beaten little cottage in a weed-grown yard. Mr. Baker began to help Father unload.

Lizza and Nat carried Sammy's cradle into the house. Mother put Sammy in it. She straightened and smiled. "What a lovely big fireplace!"

Granny sniffed. "Big enough to let the heat go up and the wind come down. Much as your life's worth to keep it wooded in the winter." She looked at Nat over her spectacles. "Think you're big enough to go fetch some fire?"

Lizza said, "I'll help!"

"You will not," Granny told her. "That's a man's work. Go along, Nat, and mind your manners."

Nat took the shovel and went down Turner's Lane to the big gloomy house with seven gables. He asked, please, could he borrow some fire?

The maid gave him a shovelful of coals. "You're mighty pindling to be carrying it. Watch you don't spill it."

"I won't spill it," Nat promised. It wasn't so easy, though, to carry the shovelful of coals and keep it level. Halfway home, he thought his arms would pull out of his shoulders.

But he got there with the fire. Mother was ready. She dumped the coals on kindling, and picking up the bellows, puffed air on the coals — gently at first — then harder. The fire sputted out in red tongues.

Nat grinned and forgot his aching arms. He dusted his hands. "There! What else can I do?"

"Help Lizza weed the yard," Granny said. "A heap of flowers there if the weeds weren't choking them."

Lizza was waiting in the yard. "What's the big secret, Nat?"

He told her about the shilling he had found, and the good-luck spell. "It's the best good-luck spell in the world. But I'll have to do it tonight, sure, while there's still a new moon."

"What if you can't see the new moon through your window?"

Nat shook his head. "That's bad luck. I'll have to wait till Hab is asleep, and then get downstairs in the dark, without knocking over anything, and come out here in the yard."

Lizza's eyes got big. "By yourself? Won't you be afraid?"

"Not very much," Nat said. "Anyway, I got to do it. Our luck's just got to change. I heard Granny talking to Mother. She's worried. She said if things don't go better now, she didn't know what we'd do." Lizza shivered. Nat added quickly. "They will go better, Lizza! Honest they will! Soon as I work my good-luck spell!"

That evening, just after supper, the wind rose, and the rain fell down the wide chimney and hissed in the fire.

Father said, "A nor'easter's brewing. We're in for three days of bad weather."

Lizza gasped. "Oh, no! If it rains . . . " She stopped. Lizza always kept a secret. She and Nat went to the window together and watched the rain slatting down in the weed-grown garden. She whispered, "Nat, there won't be any moon! What'll you do?"

Nat bit his lips. If only he hadn't gone to sleep last night! Now he'd have to wait a whole month, till another new moon, to work his good-luck spell. But he mustn't worry Lizza. Father always said boys took care of girls and women.

"I'll think of something," he promised. He said it again, to try to make it come true. "Sure, I will. I'll think of something."

CHAPTER 2

THE PRIVATEERS

The first sunny day, when Nat came down to breakfast, he still had not thought of anything to do about his good-luck spell.

Through the open window he could hear a fife and drum, and a man shouting.

Father grinned. "They're drumming up a crew for another privateer!"

"What is a privateer?" Lizza asked.

"Just any kind of ship," Father told her. "It can be a sloop, a schooner, a square-rigger. A privateer doesn't carry cargo. It carries guns. When one of our privateers sees a British ship, we capture it, and take all the Englishmen prisoners. Then we put a prize master on their ship and sail it into port and sell it — ship and cargo."

Granny said, "Pirates! That's what they are!"

Father smiled. "I guess a privateer would be a pirate

in peacetime. But this is war. We only capture English ships."

"Or get captured ourselves." Granny sniffed.

Father chuckled and got up from the table. "I think I'll walk up to the wharves and see how they're getting along."

Granny looked at him over her glasses. "Stay out of the taverns, or you'll wake up on a privateer yourself."

Father laid his hand on Granny's shoulder. "Don't worry, Mother. I've turned over a new leaf."

Granny sighed. "I hope so. But take Nat with you; then you'll be sure to come back."

"Come along, son." They walked up Derby Street toward the wharves. The fife and drum got louder.

With one hand, Nat held on to Father's hand; with the other, he clutched the shilling in his pocket. "Father, if you had more money than you ever had before in all your life, what would you do?"

"I'd invest in a privateer. I'd buy an expectation from a sailor."

"How do you buy an expectation?"

"An expectation is the money a sailor expects to make on the voyage of a privateer. You see, when we capture a British ship, we sell it. The owner of the privateer gets part of the money. The rest of it goes to the captain and crew. If you want to buy an expectation, you talk to a sailor about it. He'll take your money. Then he'll give you a slip of paper that says you'll get part of what he makes on the voyage."

"And will that be more money than you gave him?"

"Lots more."

"Why will the sailor sell his expectation, when he would have more money if he didn't?"

Father chuckled. "Here comes a sailor now. You might ask him."

Nat saw the big man coming toward them in a flat black hat, a striped jersey, and wide trousers. Before the sailor was close enough for Nat to speak to him, he saw Father.

"Captain Bowditch!" he roared. "You're just the man we need!"

Father shook his head. "You wouldn't want me on your ship. I'm a Jonah. I'd bring bad luck."

"Stow it!" the sailor roared. "You're not the only man that's lost a ship on Anguilla Reef! Come on, Captain!"

Father shook his head again. "I'm going back to my trade."

The sailor argued a while, and then went on. Nat's father stood, staring out across the blue water. He shook his head quickly, as though trying to forget something. He reached for Nat's hand and smiled. "It's better, isn't it, son, to go back to my trade?"

"Yes, Father."

"Better to be a lucky cooper than an unlucky sailor?"

"Yes, sir, Father! Lots better to be a cooper. Uh — what's a cooper?"

Father chuckled. "He makes barrels." He stared out across the water again; his smile faded. "Barrels . . . " He sighed. "Come on, Nat."

On the wharf, the crowd thickened. Father picked up Nat and carried him out on the wharf. He stopped by a sea chest and stood Nat on it. "Here's a place for you, Nat, where you can see what's going on. Whoever owns the chest won't mind. You wait here for me."

Nat promised. Father disappeared into the crowd. Nat stood on the chest and stared up at the towering masts of the ships, and the bowsprits, like long beaks, slanting into the air above him.

Men crowded the deck of the nearest ship, mounting guns. A privateer! Nat clutched his shilling and smiled.

A huge man with gray hair and a tobacco-stained grin stopped by the chest where Nat was standing. "Well, look what I've catched me!" he roared. "You shipping with me, Mate?"

Nat gulped, clutched his shilling, and tried to remember what to say. "I'm buying expectations."

The big man blinked. He rested his foot on the chest and leaned his hairy arm on his knee. "Expectations, eh? Now just what do you know about privateers?"

"I come from a long line of sea captains," Nat told him. "And I have a lot of money. I'm buying expectations."

The big man rubbed his whiskery jaw. "A lot of money, eh?"

"More money than I ever had before in all my life! More than I ever had before all put together!"

The big man sat down by Nat. "Well, Mate, we might talk business."

Nat pointed to the ship where men were mounting guns. "Are you sailing on that privateer?"

"Not that one, Mate. I'm sailing on the *Pilgrim,* out of Beverly." He motioned with his thumb. "Beverly's just across the water from here."

"Is the *Pilgrim* a good privateer?"

"Best privateer that ever raked a Britisher with a broadside! You want to buy expectations from me?"

Nat's heart pounded so hard he could not talk, but he nodded.

The big man took off his flat black hat and fished a paper from the crown. "Just got one left. For ten per cent of my expectations. What'll you give me for it?"

"All my money!" Nat laid his shilling in the big man's hand.

The big man stared at the shilling. "Well, I'll be a copper-bottomed, bevel-edged . . . Most money you ever had, eh?"

"Yes, sir!"

"And you come from a long line of sea captains? Who are you?"

"Nat Bowditch."

"Captain Bowditch's boy, eh? I remember when the *Polly* went aground. Same day the war started. April 19, 1775."

"Granny said it 'took the tuck' out of Father." Nat told the big man about his good-luck spell that he was going to work, only the nor'easter came, and hid the moon.

The big man rubbed his bristling chin. He looked at the shilling. "It's a bargain, Mate. But keep it a secret! Don't ever tell any man that Tom Perry sold a tenth of his expectations for a shilling! They'd stow me in the brig. What's worse, they'd put me on the binnacle list!"

Nat didn't know what he was talking about, but he promised. "I'll tell no man!" He took the slip of paper, folded it, and put it in his pocket.

Tom Perry stood. He flipped the shilling into the air, caught it, and grinned. "I'll drink to our success, Mate!" He ambled away, his big shoulders making holes in the crowd.

Nat sat on the chest and waited for his father. A secret!

He must tell no man! But he could tell Lizza. Lizza always kept a secret. He'd have to have someone to talk to. If he didn't, he'd burst! Just think! Nat Bowditch — with a share in a privateer! His chest felt too big for his ribs.

When Nat and Father got home, Nat found Lizza weeding the garden. He showed her the paper, and told her about Tom Perry.

"Oh, Nat! That's wonderful! How soon will you get your money?"

"I don't know. Let's ask Father." They went in the house.

Father smiled. "How long before a privateer comes back? It all depends. Maybe in a few months, maybe in a year, maybe longer."

Granny sniffed. "And maybe never."

Nat and Lizza went back to the garden. Lizza whispered, "A year! Maybe two years!"

"Maybe never."

Lizza said, "Granny's just a little — well — fussy about the ocean. You're not worrying, are you, Nat?"

Nat squared his shoulders. "No, not a bit worried. Not a bit." But he looked at his slip of paper, and wondered.

CHAPTER 3

WORD FROM THE *PILGRIM*

The weeks passed and months. No word from Tom Perry. Time came to start to school.

Lizza said, "I'm glad I'm not going. They say Master Watson is grouchy. Are you scared about going to school, Nat?"

Nat shook his head. "No, I'm not scared . . . very much."

But when he and Hab entered the schoolhouse, and Master Watson bristled his eyebrows at them, Nat's knees began to shake.

Master Watson glared at Nat. "What's he doing here?"

"He's just little for his age, Master Watson," Hab said. "He's gone to school two years in Danvers."

Master Watson snorted. "A dame school! Women!" He glared at Nat again. "Sit over there with the young ones. And keep still!"

"Yes, sir." Nat climbed on a bench and sat.

Hour after hour, all morning, he sat and listened. When they came back in the afternoon, he sat and listened again. If only he could answer a question the very first day! Then Master Watson wouldn't glare at him because he was little.

Three times that day Nat knew an answer. But before he could get his hand up, someone else answered the question.

It was almost time for school to let out. Through the window, Nat heard a fife shrilling and the thud of a drum. Another privateer was making ready for sea. They were drumming up a crew!

Master Watson's voice broke in on Nat's thoughts. "What happened on April 19, 1775?"

At last! He could answer that question! Nat stood up on the bench and waved his hand. "I know! I know!"

Master Watson's eyebrows bristled. "Well? Speak up!"

Nat took a deep breath. "On April 19, 1775, my father's sloop, *Polly*, went aground on Anguilla Reef. And — "

Nat stopped with a gasp. Master Watson had grabbed his shoulders and was shaking him.

Jerkily, through the shaking, Nat heard Hab's voice. "It's true, Master Watson! Nat wasn't trying to be smart!"

Nat didn't remember anything else until Master Watson said, "School is dismissed!" And he was outside, walking up the street with Hab.

"Hab, what was the matter? What I said was true. It was the right answer!"

Hab tried to explain. The Battle of Lexington was

very important. When anyone asked about April 19, 1775, the Battle of Lexington would be the right answer — no matter what else happened on that day.

Nat said, "Huh! I like arithmetic better. Two plus two is four. Always. Nobody's going to shake you when you say that."

Hab chuckled. "That's it, Nat. You stick to arithmetic. He'll never shake you for that."

But Master Watson did not give arithmetic problems to boys Nat's size. Not real ones. Every problem Nat got he could work in his head.

Maybe next year, he thought, I'll get bigger problems. Big enough to work on my slate. Maybe next year will be more fun at school.

But next year wasn't more fun. Nat had to go to school alone. Hab was twelve, now, and he stopped school to help Father make barrels. Their luck had not changed.

One day Nat sighed as he watched Master Watson put a nice, long problem on a big boy's slate. He held up his hand. "Please, sir, could I have one of those big problems, too?"

Master Watson glared. "No! You're too little! I haven't time to bother with you!"

That night after supper Father said, "What's the matter, son?"

"Master Watson won't give me big problems to work on my slate, just little ones I can do in my head."

Father chuckled. "First time I ever heard a boy complain about that! We'll see what we can do!" He brought paper and ink to the table, and sharpened a quill. He wrote a note, and dusted it with sand to dry the ink.

"Here you are. How does this sound?" He read:

Master Watson
 My son, Nat, likes arithmetic. Will you please give him bigger problems to work?
Your obedient servant
HABAKKUK BOWDITCH

The next day Master Watson read the note and scowled. He grabbed Nat's slate and pencil. The pencil went *squeak, squeak,* filling half the slate with a problem.

"There! That will keep you busy for a while!"

Nat hurried to his seat and worked the problem. When he had the answer, he checked it over to be sure it was right. He grinned. The answer came out the same both times. That's what he liked about arithmetic. He carried his slate to Master Watson's desk. "Please sir, may I have another problem?"

Master Watson snorted. "Too hard for you, eh? No, you may not have another problem! Work on that one until you get the answer!"

"But I've got the answer!"

"Eh?" Master Watson grabbed the slate and checked the problem. "Who helped you?"

"No one!"

Master Watson slapped his hand down on his desk. "Don't lie to me! Who helped you?"

Nat forgot about being afraid of Master Watson. He clenched his fists and yelled, "I don't tell lies!"

Master Watson grabbed up his ruler. For a long time

he stared at Nat. Then he spoke through his teeth. "You have until tomorrow to tell me the truth. Tomorrow, if you don't tell me who helped you, I'll give you a whaling you'll never forget!"

That night at supper Granny said, "Eat your supper, Nat."

But Nat couldn't seem to swallow. He chewed and chewed each bite until it somehow went away.

After supper, Hab said, "What's the matter, Nat?"

Nat told him about the problem. "I didn't think he'd ever scold me about arithmetic, but he did."

Hab squared his shoulders and stuck out his lower lip. "Don't worry, Nat. I'll take care of that. In the morning!"

The next morning he marched to school with Nat. "Master Watson," he said, "Nat can't help it if he likes arithmetic."

Master Watson snapped, "He never worked that problem that fast without help! And no one can make me believe he did!"

"Why don't you give him another one," Hab asked, "and stand right over him while he works it?"

"I'll do that very thing." Master Watson snatched the slate. This time the problem covered almost all of one side. "All right, work that! Right here at my desk, where I can keep an eye on you!"

Nat shivered. The numbers on the slate jiggled but he gulped and began to work. He could feel Master Watson's eyes glaring down at him. After a little, though, he forgot all about Master Watson. His own problem! A big one. And it would come out right.

Arithmetic always did. Swiftly he worked, finished it, checked it, and looked up.

"There!"

Master Watson stared with his mouth open. "I — I — it's hard to believe — even when you see it happen." He held out his hand. "Nat, I'm sorry about yesterday. Will you shake hands on it?"

"Yes, sir. And please may I have another problem?"

"What!"

Hab said, "Look, Nat, Master Watson can't spend all day writing problems for you!"

"It's all right. I'll give him another problem." Master Watson shook his head again. "I never saw anything like it. Nat, if you knew half as much Latin as you know arithmetic, you could enter Harvard tomorrow!"

That night at supper Nat asked, "What's Harvard?"

Mother and Father chuckled. Granny said, "Oldest college in the country. Whatever made you think of Harvard?"

Hab told them what Master Watson had said.

Mother beamed and hugged Nat. "That's wonderful, Nat. And you shall go to college. Some day you'll be a Harvard man."

Granny said, "He might as well; never going to be sizable enough to handle a ship. Come a gale at sea, you'd have to ballast his feet. Takes a heap of money, though, to go to Harvard."

"When the war's over, times will get better," Mother said.

Lizza rolled her eyes at Nat. He knew she was thinking about his expectation. When Tom Perry came back, Nat would have plenty of money for Harvard.

After supper he and Lizza walked down Turner's
Lane and out on the wharf.

Lizza said, "I wish Tom Perry would come."

"He will, some day."

"But, Nat, how will you know where to find him?"

"He'll find me," Nat said. "He knows my name."

The spring Nat was eight, Granny said, "You know
where Dr. Stearns' apothecary shop is, Nat?"

Mother said, "Nonsense, dear. I'm all right. We can't
afford — "

"We can't afford to lose you." Granny wrote something on a piece of paper and said, "Take this to Dr.
Stearns, Nat."

Nat felt a cold lump in his stomach. He ran all the
way to Dr. Stearns' shop, and gave him the paper. "It's
medicine! For Mother! Please hurry!"

"No cause to worry, Nat. It's just a tonic." Dr. Stearns
gave Nat the *Salem Gazette*. "Read this, why don't you,
while you wait."

Nat looked at the paper. The first thing that caught
his eye was the word Pilgrim. He read the advertisement:

At BEVERLY
That copper-bottom, fast-sailing, frigate-built ship,
MARS . . . captured by the PILGRIM, Joseph Robinson,
Commander,
Will be sold Wednesday, 11, instant, at 10 o'clock.

Nat carried the paper to Dr. Stearns. "When's 'eleven
instant'?"

"Eleventh of this month." He glanced at the paper. "Reading about the auction of the *Mars,* eh? Did you ever see the auction of a prize ship?"

"No, sir."

"It's a sale. There's a man they call the 'auctioneer.' He puts everything up for sale. Whoever offers the most money gets whatever the auctioneer is selling right then. That's going to be quite a sale. Captain Robinson will make a pretty penny from the *Mars.*"

Nat said, "I have a friend on the *Pilgrim.* Tom Perry."

"That so? Well, your friend Tom Perry will make a pretty penny, too. I'll be over at Beverly for the auction. I'll ask about him." He gave Nat a packet. "There's the medicine, Nat."

The cold lump came back in Nat's stomach. He ran all the way home. He watched anxiously while Mother mixed a dose and took it. "Do you feel better now?"

"Much better, dear." Mother smiled. "It's nasty enough to make anyone well!"

Nat sighed with relief and ran to tell Lizza about the auction of the *Mars.* "Next week, on the twelfth, we'll go to Dr. Stearns' shop. He'll have news about Tom Perry!"

On the afternoon of the twelfth, Lizza and Nat got the paper from its hiding place and hurried up the street.

"Nat, what will you get first with all your money?"

"A new ship for Father — bigger than the *Polly.* And then presents for everybody else."

"What will you get for you?"

"I'm going to save my money to go to Harvard."

"Oh, Nat!" Lizza smiled and squeezed his hand.

Nat smiled, too. "Did I tell you what Tom Perry called me? He called me 'Mate.'"

When they got to the apothecary shop, Dr. Stearns was busy talking to the Reverend Dr. Prince and Dr. Holyoke. A big stack of books was on the counter, and the men were looking at them.

Dr. Holyoke said, "You can't tear pages out of these books to wrap your drugs in!"

The apothecary shrugged. "Paper's scarce!"

"But these books are priceless!"

Dr. Stearns rubbed his chin and smiled. "I tell you what. If you want these books, I'll sell them to you for just what I paid for them at the auction: one hundred and fifty-eight pounds and ten shillings."

"In hard money?" Dr. Prince asked.

"No, in continental currency."

Dr. Holyoke said, "In hard money, not quite forty pounds. Will you give us a week to raise the money?"

The apothecary pursed his lips. "Well, yes — but I may use a few pages here and there to wrap a few drugs . . ."

Dr. Holyoke roared, "Don't you dare touch a page!"

Dr. Stearns laughed and promised. When the men had gone, he said, "Well, hello there, Nat — and Lizza! I didn't see you!"

"Did you find out about my friend Tom Perry?"

"Yes, Nat." He came from behind his counter, up-ended a box, and sat down. "A friend of yours, was he?"

"Yes, sir. A good friend. He called me 'Mate.'"

"Then you can be mighty proud of him, Nat. He died a hero. It happened almost a year ago. The *Pilgrim's* men were boarding an English ship. It was close, hand-to-hand fighting. A Britisher leveled a gun at the *Pilgrim's* first mate. Tom Perry leaped for the man. He caught the gun blast full in his chest. They buried him at sea — a hero."

Nat's throat ached. His tongue felt dry. He licked his lips. "Thank you for finding out for me."

Slowly Nat and Lizza went back to Turner's Lane. They walked out on the wharf and stared across the endless, empty water.

Lizza whispered, "It's wonderful to have a friend that was a hero, Nat. To have him call you 'Mate' and everything."

Nat swallowed hard.

After a little, Lizza said, "Nat, did you ever hear about what fishermen's people do when a fisherman dies and is buried at sea? The people at home scatter flowers on the water to remember him by."

Nat pulled the slip of paper from his pocket. Slowly he tore it in tiny pieces and let them fall in the water.

Lizza whispered, "If you squinch your eyes, it looks just exactly like little flowers . . . almost . . ." She squeezed his hand. "Times will get better, Nat — when the war's over."

Nat shivered. No expectation now. No new ship for Father, no presents. No money to go to Harvard. Nothing.

Lizza whispered, "Good-by, Tom Perry."

Nat said, "Good-by." He was saying good-by to a lot of things.

CHAPTER 4

"BOYS DON'T BLUBBER"

A few days later Nat came out of school one afternoon and found Hab waiting for him. "Come on, Nat. I'm going to show you a new kind of ship. She's the *Freedom*."

Out on the wharf men were trundling boxes and bales of cargo to the *Freedom*.

"She isn't a privateer," Nat said. "She's carrying cargo." Then he saw guns mounted on the deck.

"She's a letter of marque ship," Hab said. "She carries cargo, but she can fight if she has to." Hab straightened. "I'm signed on her crew, Nat."

Nat gulped. "Does Mother know? And Father?"

"Sure, they all know. They understand. After all, I come from a long line of sea captains, don't I? And I'm big for my age."

"I'm growing," Nat said. He grinned. "I bet next winter I'll be too big for my coat, and William will get it." Nat remembered last winter when Hab had out-grown his coat. "Did you get cold last winter, Hab?"

"Plenty cold."

Nat was puzzled. "But when the boys yelled at you, you always said, 'I'm not cold. Only sissies need winter coats.' "

"Of course." Hab frowned. "Boys don't blubber. If something hurts, you say it doesn't." He looked up at the tall masts of the *Freedom* and grinned. "She's a grand ship, isn't she?"

Nat's stomach felt hollow. What would it be like with Hab gone? But boys didn't blubber. He bit his lips to steady them and squared his shoulders. "Yes, Hab. A grand ship. How — how — long before you sail?"

Hab shrugged and looked important. "We can't tell. The British are trying to blockade the harbor. They've got ships offshore there, all the time, watching for our ships."

"What — what — would happen if they'd catch the *Freedom?*"

Hab shrugged again. "They won't."

Nat shivered.

A few mornings later, when he awakened, Hab was gone. He'd left a note for Nat:

Dear Nat

It's foggy tonight, so we're going to sail. Tomorrow, the British will still be watching for us, but we'll be gone. You're the oldest boy now. Remember, boys don't blubber.

Yours sincerely,
HAB

Nat scrambled into his clothes and hurried downstairs and out of the house. He ran toward the wharf. The *Freedom* was gone. Nat turned from the wharf, back into town, and climbed a little hill. He looked toward the sea. The fog had cleared. Had the *Freedom* escaped from the English ship? Or had she been captured? How long would it be before they'd know what happened? A year? Two years?

At the breakfast table, everyone talked fast, and tried to sound cheerful.

"I think the war's almost over," Father said. "That's what the shipowners think, too. You can tell. That's why they're sending out letter of marque ships now. If a privateer's at sea when the war ends, she'll have her voyage for nothing. But a letter of marque ship will go right on about her business, carrying cargo, buying and selling, making money for her owner . . . Making money hand over fist."

Nat knew Father was thinking about Elias Derby. He was one of the richest shipowners in Salem. People said he was one of the richest men in the country.

"If the war's almost over, will things get better now?" Lizza asked.

Father nodded. "Of course. Just any day now."

But things didn't get better. All summer prices climbed higher and higher and food got scarcer and scarcer. Sometimes Mother and Granny did not have anything to cook but potatoes, three meals a day.

In the fall, Hab came back. He was brown as an Indian. Granny said he had grown a foot in every direction.

"Did the *Freedom* have any fights?" Nat asked.

Hab shook his head and grinned. "Not a fight! The English can't catch her; she's too fast for them. Don't worry about the *Freedom*, Nat."

But a week later, when Hab sailed again, Nat did worry. Would the *Freedom* escape? How long before they'd know?

Then one morning Nat wakened suddenly to hear bells clanging and men shouting. Everybody in the house was stirring.

"I wonder what's wrong?" Mother said.

"It's a bad wreck, or a bad fire," Father said as he hurried to open the door.

Outside men were shouting, "Cornwallis is taken! We've won the war! Hoorraaaay. Cornwallis is taken!"

For a moment everybody stood and stared; then they all began to laugh and talk at the same time. Father hugged Mother and Granny, Nat hugged Mary and Lizza, William and Sammy jumped up and down and yelled, even Lois, the baby, squealed.

After breakfast Nat and Lizza went with Father to watch the cheering, shouting crowds. When they neared Derby Wharf, they saw a tall, soldierly-looking man come out of one of the warehouses. The crowd cheered him.

Nat said, "Is he a general or something?"

"He's Captain John Derby," Father said. "Back in 1775, when the war started with the Battle of Lexington, the Americans wanted to get word to England just as fast as they could. They knew the King's messenger would sail in the fastest ship he could find to tell the story of the battle the way the English soldiers wanted it told. The Americans wanted to reach England first with their side of the story. The problem was to find a ship that was fast enough and a captain that was daring enough to reach England ahead of the English messenger. So, of course, they turned to Salem. They knew we had the finest ships and the best sailors in the country. Elias Derby's ship, the *Quero,* carried the message. And Captain John Derby was the man that got the word to London."

"Did he get there first — before the King's messengers?" Lizza asked.

Father stared at her. "Lizza! What a question! Of course he got there first! Isn't he a Salem man?"

Then Father grinned and Lizza giggled. She said, "Now things will get better, won't they?"

"Of course they will!"

But prices went right on climbing; paper money was worth less and less. For a while it took ten paper dollars to equal one silver dollar, then twenty, then forty. Finally one hundred paper dollars would not buy a dollar's worth of food. And prices were still climbing. Corn, that used to cost a few shillings a bushel, cost twenty-five dollars a bushel — in silver. In paper money, two thousand dollars would not buy a bushel of corn.

When winter came, Nat had outgrown his coat. He remembered what Hab had told him, and sometimes, when the boys jeered at him, he said, "I'm not cold. Only sissies need winter coats." Sometimes he just shrugged and didn't say anything. He was afraid if he tried to talk his teeth would chatter. Over and over he told himself, Boys don't blubber; that's the main thing. He thought of what people had said. When the war was

over, times would get better. Why didn't they? He asked
Father about it.

"When peace comes," Father said, "things will get
better."

"But the war's over, isn't it? Hasn't peace come?"

Father said, "The fighting has stopped, but they
haven't settled the peace terms yet. That's what John
Adams and some of the other men are doing in Paris now,
talking over the peace terms."

"I hope they hurry up about it," Nat said.

Months went by, a year passed, and finally in the spring
of '83, almost a year and a half after the fighting had
stopped, General Washington proclaimed the peace.

Again Salem was the proudest town in the country.
Salem's Captain John Derby brought news of the peace
to America. He had been in Paris when the first terms
of the peace treaty were settled.

"And he crowded sail," Father said, "and brought the
news of the peace from Paris in twenty-two days! That
takes nerve!"

Nat said, "Why does it take nerve to crowd sail?"

"The more sail you carry, the faster you go," Father
told him. "But you have to watch out. If the wind rises
suddenly, and blows hard against all that spread of sail,
it can snap your masts."

"Was that how you lost the *Polly?*" Nat asked. "Were
you crowding sail?"

Father shook his head. "No. A storm drove me on a
lee shore, and I lost my anchor to windward." For a moment he was silent. "The windward side of a ship is the
side the wind's coming from. The lee side is the other

side of the ship. If a storm drives you toward land on your lee side, that's about the most dangerous thing that can happen to you. Your ship has to 'claw off' that lee shore — fight against the storm. If your ship can't claw off, then you'll heave an anchor to windward, to try to hold the ship where she is. That's your last chance to save her. If you lose your anchor to windward . . . " He stopped talking and sat a moment, staring at nothing. He sighed and stood. "Well, I'd better get back to making barrels." He left the house.

Lizza was big-eyed. "Wrecked on a reef!"

Nat said, "And that took the tuck out of Father, when he lost the *Polly*."

Granny bristled. "Who said so?"

"You did. I heard you tell Mother."

Granny eyed Nat over her spectacles. "Humph. Why don't you and Lizza go and watch the celebrating?"

They held hands and ran up Derby Street. Lizza gasped when the guns in Salem Harbor fired salutes and the cannon on the forts boomed an answer.

The sailors were celebrating louder than anyone else. One big sailor got up on a barrel and yelled questions. The others roared the answers.

"Who won this war?" he yelled.

"We did! The privateers of Salem!"

Lizza squeezed Nat's hand. "Look! Captain Derby!"

Nat saw the tall, soldierly man crossing the street toward Derby Wharf. The sailor on the barrel saw him, too. He pointed.

"Who took the news of Lexington to England?"

The crowd yelled, "Captain John Derby!"

"Who brought the news of the peace to America?"

"Captain John Derby! Of Salem! Greatest city in America!"

Someone yelled, "New York's the greatest! Salem's next!"

A fight started. But· Captain John Derby roared, " 'Vast there! To the Ship's Tavern, and splice the main brace!"

The cheering, yelling men shoved each other and followed him to the tavern.

Lizza sighed. "Isn't he wonderful, Nat? Isn't everything wonderful? Now the war's over and times will get better!"

But times didn't get better. Prices went right on climbing. When school was out, Nat helped his father in the cooperage. All summer he worked "from can-see to can't-see." Sometimes at night he was almost too tired to eat his supper. He was going to be glad, he thought, when school started again.

The night before school was to start, Father said, "You'll have to mind the shop tomorrow, Nat. I have to go over to Beverly."

Nat's stomach felt hollow. "But — but — school starts tomorrow."

"I know. But I need you, Nat."

"But — but — I thought — when school started again . . ."

His father did not look at Nat. "Maybe, when times are better, you can go back. Right now, I need you." He picked up his hat. "I'll be back in a little while," he said.

No more school! Nat sat in a daze. The room swam in front of his eyes.

At nine o'clock, Father had not come back. Granny muttered under her breath and snapped at the children. At last everyone had gone to bed but Mother and Granny and Nat.

Mother said, "Nat, would you like to take a walk with me?"

Granny looked up sharply. "You've no business out in the night air."

Mother smiled. "Nonsense. I'm all right."

She and Nat went out into the dark, moonless night, and walked down Turner's Lane and out on the wharf. Mother helped Nat find the North Star, and told him how the Big Dipper swung around it, and how to tell time by the Dipper. Then she was silent, standing with her hand on Nat's shoulder, looking up at the stars.

Boys don't blubber. He must remember that. Finally Nat said, "It's all right about school, Mother. When times are better, I'll get to go back."

Mother did not answer. She was still gazing up at the sky. After a while she said, "I made up a sort of saying for myself, Nat. *I will lift up my eyes unto the stars.* Sometimes, if you look at the stars long enough, it helps. It shrinks your day-by-day troubles down to size." She smiled. "We'd better go back. Granny and Father will be wondering where we are."

When they got back to the house, Granny was still alone. She said, "Where'd you go?"

Mother said, "Nowhere. Just to look at the stars."

"You beat all." Granny shook her head. "I wonder where he is."

"He feels bad about keeping Nat out of school," Mother said.

Granny sighed. "Rum won't help. If he put more rum in barrels and less in . . . " She stopped. The wind began to rise. Granny shivered. "Going to be an early winter."

CHAPTER 5

A VOICE IN THE NIGHT

It was an early winter. A nor'easter howled in from the Atlantic, bringing rain that changed to sleet and then to snow. Nat hugged his thin coat about him and scurried back from an errand. The sleet lashed his face and brought tears to his eyes, so that he could not see where he was going. He ran into a man, stumbled and lost his balance. He went down in the mud and slush. "Excuse me," he said. He looked up and recognized the roly-poly man. He gasped, "Excuse me, sir!"

It was the new pastor of East Church — Dr. Bentley. Everyone said Dr. Bentley was about the brightest man who had ever come to Salem. They said he knew twenty languages!

Dr. Bentley helped Nat to his feet, took out a handkerchief, and wiped at the mud on Nat's clothes. "No, no. Excuse me. You're the one who tumbled." He must have noticed how thin Nat's coat was. He said, "This cold spell took a man by surprise, didn't it? No time to get his winter coat out of the garret."

Nat's answer was always ready. "I don't get cold; only sissies need winter coats." Then he saw the heavy coat that bundled Dr. Bentley. "I — I — mean — when you're young, you know. Of course when a man gets old, I guess he needs a heavy coat. I — I — mean — "

Dr. Bentley chuckled. "That's right. Old fellows of twenty-five — like me — have to watch their health." He walked along toward the cooperage with Nat. "You're Nathaniel Bowditch, aren't you? I've heard Master Watson talk about you. You're not in school today?"

"I've quit school to help my father."

Dr. Bentley stared at him. "What? But that's — that's — " He stopped. After a while he said, "I'll leave you here, Nat. Good-by."

When Nat got home that evening, Lizza was big-eyed. When she had a chance, she whispered, "Dr. Bentley came to see Mother! He told her you ought to be getting ready for Harvard right now! Isn't that wonderful? When a man as bright as Dr. Bentley says you're bright, too?"

"What did Mother say?"

"She thanked him! And she smiled and smiled. After he had gone, she didn't smile, though. She walked back and forth. And Granny said 'Stop stewing about that boy and take care of yourself.' "

Something colder than a nor'easter settled in Nat's chest. "Granny's worried about Mother."

Lizza nodded slowly. "I know. But Mother always

laughs and says 'I'm all right.' She said that today. She said, 'I'll live to see Nat a Harvard man.' "

Not quite three months later, just before Christmas, Mother died.

The night after the funeral, Father sat at the table with his head in his hands. "I'll do better, Mother," he said. "I swear I will."

Granny's eyes were sad. "I hope so, son. But you'd better claw off that lee shore. You've lost your anchor to windward."

Mary put her arm around Granny. "Why don't you go to bed, dear?"

Granny sighed. "I think I will. Seems like I've lost my tuck."

Not quite two years later, when Nat was twelve, Granny died.

Again Father sat by the table with his head in his hands. Again he said, "I'll do better, Mary. I swear I will."

Mary didn't answer. She just looked at Father. Her eyes were sad as Granny's used to be.

Nat knew what she was thinking. "You've lost your last anchor to windward."

Two months later, something wakened Nat in the night. He raised up on one scrawny elbow and stared into the dark. What was it? He listened. There were only the sounds he had known all these years in Salem — the creaking of the old wooden house, buffeted by Atlantic winds. No other sounds. But something had wakened him. He shivered, and started to huddle down under the blanket again. Then he heard his father's voice. Father must be talking to Mary. Since Mother and Granny were gone, they all turned to Mary.

At first Father's voice was only a rumble. Then Nat heard the scrape of a chair and the thud of a log being pitched on the fire.

For a moment Father's voice was louder. "I think it's the thing for Nat. He's not much good in the cooperage; he's better with his head than his hands. He won't be bringing in any money, but there will be one less mouth to feed. Master Watson always said he was bright. And I talked to Michael Walsh. He said . . . "

The chair scraped again. Father's voice died to a rumble. Nat could no longer hear what he was saying. But he had heard enough to know what they were talking about. Michael Walsh was a teacher!

Nat sat up again. The covers fell away, but he did not notice the cold. He was going to go back to school! He must be going away somewhere to school. Father had said, "One less mouth to feed."

Surprised, Nat found tears on his face and wiped them with the back of his hand. "That's funny," he said. "I don't cry. Boys don't blubber."

Silly to cry when he was happy enough to burst. He was going back to school! Where — he didn't know — but somewhere. And after he had learned all he could in that school, he'd go to Harvard. How, he didn't know. He just knew that he would. Latin — he'd have to learn Latin to go to Harvard. Maybe that was why he was going away somewhere to school. So he could learn Latin to get ready for Harvard.

When he got to Harvard, Nat told himself, he'd work

hard — harder than he had ever worked in his life. When he finished Harvard, his father could come to his graduation. Mary, too. And Lizza. Maybe the whole family!

Father would say, "Nat, I did the right thing when I took you out of the cooperage and put you back to book learning. As a cooper, you're a good Latin scholar."

And they'd laugh together. Nat wished he could jump out of bed now and go talk to his father about it — tell him what he had heard. But that wouldn't be fair. This was Father's surprise. He must have the fun of telling it. Tomorrow, at breakfast, that was when Father would tell him. Tell him he was going back to school!

Smiling, Nat lay down again. For a long time he lay there, too full of plans to go to sleep.

The next morning when he wakened, it was late. Only Father and Mary were at the table. As Nat ate his breakfast, he watched his Father's face for some sign of a twinkle to show he was thinking about the surprise. But Father frowned over a paper he was studying and never looked up. Nat glanced toward Mary, to see if she showed a twinkle. But Mary looked pale, as though she hadn't slept very well.

At last Father pushed back his chair and cleared his throat. "Er — Nat . . . "

It was coming now! "Yes, Father?"

"I've been thinking a lot about you, Nat. You know, I believe you'll do better with your head than with your hands."

"I think so, too." Nat couldn't keep from grinning.

Father said, "I've been talking to Jonathan Hodges about you. You know — of Ropes and Hodges."

Nat said, "I know who he is." Mr. Hodges must be the one that talked Father into sending Nat back to school. Father would pay attention to what Mr. Hodges said. Everyone talked about how well Ropes and Hodges were doing. Just twenty-one or so, both of them, and they had the biggest ship chandlery in Salem. Nat had been in the chandlery — a long wooden building on Neptune Street, near Union Wharf. The chandlery was crammed with everything for ships — everything from barrels of salt beef to cables and marline-spikes. Yes, Father would pay attention to what Mr. Hodges said.

Father frowned and seemed to be hunting for words. "Er — ah — Jonathan Hodges thinks you show a good bit of promise, Nat. He thinks a couple of months — maybe three — under Michael Walsh will give you just what you need."

Two months under Michael Walsh — or three. Nat tried to figure it out. Mr. Walsh was right here in town. Father had said there would be "one less mouth to feed."

Father said, "Mr. Hodges knows you're quick at figures. He says Mr. Walsh can teach you enough bookkeeping in two or three months. Then Ropes and Hodges will sign your papers." He looked at the paper he had been studying and then handed it to Nat. Nat began to read:

INDENTURE
This indenture witnesseth that
NATHANIEL BOWDITCH
hath put himself, and, by these Presents, doth
voluntarily and of his own free will and accord, and
with the consent of

HABAKKUK BOWDITCH
put and bind himself apprentice to
ROPES AND HODGES
to learn the Art, Trade or Mystery of
SHIP CHANDLERY
for and during a term of NINE YEARS.

Nat picked up the paper and held it in front of his face. *Nine years!* Until he was twenty-one! For nine years he would belong to the Ship Chandlery of Ropes and Hodges. For nine years! The paper blurred in front of his eyes. He caught a sentence here and there: "During all which said term the said apprentice NATHANIEL BOWDITCH shall faithfully serve . . . He shall not absent himself by Day or Night from the same Ropes and Hodges Service without leave . . . "

He'd live there, too. That was what Father had meant. "No money," he had said, "just one less mouth to feed." *He'd live there.* In two months — or three — just as soon as he knew enough bookkeeping — he'd leave home and go to live with Mr. Ropes or Mr. Hodges. For nine years *he would not leave by Day or Night without permission.*

Father said, "Well, Nat, what do you think?"

Nat stole a glance from behind the paper toward Mary. Poor Mary, she looked so worried. Hab had said boys took care of girls and women. Kept them from worrying.

Nat managed to grin. "I think I'll do better with bookkeeping than barrel staves, all right. There's just one part of this that bothers me."

"Yes, Nat?"

"It says here I must not contract matrimony. After all, when a man is twelve . . . "

Mary said, "Oh, Nat, you simpleton!" Her laugh was shaky, but she did laugh.

Nat got up quickly. "I think I'll hurry right over to Mr. Walsh's."

He whistled while he found his slate and pencil. He whistled until he was out of the house and up the street. Then the whistle died.

All the way to Mr. Walsh's house Nat's feet seemed to beat out the words: Nine years . . . nine years . . . nine years . . .

Two or three months to study bookkeeping. Then no more school — ever.

Indentured: Nathaniel Bowditch.

CHAPTER 6

"SAIL BY ASH BREEZE!"

When Nat had been studying bookkeeping for two weeks, Michael Walsh said, "You're coming along fine, Nat." He smiled. "It isn't going to take you any three months to be ready for Ropes and Hodges! Two months — and you'll be a bookkeeper!"

"Thank you, Mr. Walsh." Heartsick, Nat said good night and started home. Only six more weeks until he'd leave home. Only six more weeks, and then for nine years he could never leave the chandlery or Mr. Hodges' house without permission.

Lizza came to meet him. "Look, Nat!" she whispered. She showed him an advertisement she had found in a *Salem Gazette:*

SIXTY DOLLARS REWARD
   Ran away from the subscriber on Monday night the 4th, two indented apprentices . . .

Whoever will take up either or both of said runaways, and return them to the subscriber or secure them in any way shall have a reward of 30 dollars for each.

All persons are forbid harboring or trusting said runaways . . .

"See, Nat?" she whispered. "Being indentured is just like being in jail. If you run away, someone will c-c-capture you and bring you b-b-back."

Nat's mouth felt dry, but he managed to smile. "But I'm not going to run away, Lizza. What would I want tc run away for? I'm going to learn a trade. Come on, we'd better hurry. I have a lot of studying to do after supper."

After they had eaten, Nat spread his work on the table. William and Sammy brought their slates and sat by him, one on each side. Mary worked at her spinning wheel; Lizza knitted a sock. Little Lois bit her tongue and studied her *New England Primer*.

Nat looked around him. His home. His family. In just a little while . . . He tried to swallow the lump in his throat.

William said, "I want a problem, Nat. A big one."

Nat took his slate. "Sure, William. You want one, too, Sammy?" He put problems on both their slates.

For a while there was no sound in the room but the click of Lizza's knitting needles, the hum of Mary's spinning wheel, the squeak of the slate pencils, and the drowsy song Lois was making out of a verse in her *New England Primer:*

> *The Moon gives light*
> *In time of night.*

She sang it over and over, to a tune of her own.

Only six more weeks at home. For a moment the work in front of Nat blurred. He blinked, swallowed hard, and began working again. Maybe Mr. Walsh would change his mind. Maybe after two months he'd say, "I think you'd better have another month, Nat." Maybe . . .

But on Friday at the end of Nat's two months, Mr. Hodges came to Michael Walsh's school. Mr. Hodges was a tall, sandy-haired young man, with a long face that looked stern until he smiled. He smiled now at Nat.

"Well, Mr. Walsh, how's Nat getting along? Had he better have another month of training? After all, a lad of twelve — "

Mr. Walsh beamed. "No, indeed! He's amazing! No reason at all to keep him here another month."

Nat's heart sank.

Mr. Hodges said, "Fine. Then, Nat, suppose you come along with me. We'll get you settled in your new home, and then you can begin to get acquainted at the chandlery."

Nat gulped. He said good-by to Mr. Walsh and followed Mr. Hodges out the door.

Presently Mr. Hodges stopped in front of a big, square house. "Here we are." He led the way inside, and up the stairs to the garret. He opened a door. "This will be your room, Nat."

Through a blur of tears Nat saw a narrow bed with a patchwork quilt, a washstand with a bowl and pitcher, a small table, and a chair.

"I think you'll like it," Mr. Hodges said. "You'll have a good view of the harbor."

Nat went to the window and stared hard at the ships until the blurred outlines cleared and he could see masts and rigging.

Mr. Hodges checked the wardrobe and the chest of drawers. "Everything is cleared out and ready for your clothes."

"I have them on," Nat said. "Most of them."

For a moment, Mr. Hodges looked stern; then he smiled. "You'll be getting more clothes, Nat. You see, we have a bargain with you. You keep books for us; we furnish you board, room, and clothes, and teach you the 'trade, art, or mystery' of ship chandlery." He chuckled. "Sometimes I'm not sure which it is — a trade, an art, or a mystery. Do you think this room will — you'll be happy here?"

Nat turned quickly to the window and stared hard at the ships again. Presently he said, "Yes, sir, this will be fine."

"Then suppose we go down to the chandlery and look around."

When they reached the long wooden building on Neptune Street, a lanky, unshaven man lounged against the door. He said, "Morning, Mr. Hodges. Mr. Ropes had to go on an errand. He asked me to keep an eye on things till you got back."

Mr. Hodges said, "This is Ben Meeker, Nat. Ben, this is Nat Bowditch, our new apprentice. Suppose you take one of our catalogues, and show Nat where everything is." He pulled two copies of a little flat notebook, about two by five inches, from his pocket, and gave one to Nat and one to Ben.

On the cover Nat read, "Catalogue of Ropes and

Hodges — Ship Chandlers." He opened the notebook. The pages were blank, excepting for a single column of words down the middle. Everything seemed to be listed there — from hardtack to copper nails — from sextants to coffeepots.

Mr. Hodges said, "Plenty of blank space, isn't there? That's so a man can mark his order right in the catalogue — so many barrels of this — so many pounds of that. It saves him the bother of writing out his order." He chuckled. "And it saves us the bother of trying to read his writing. All right, Ben, show Nat around."

Ben yawned, stretched, and led the way through the shop to where huge coils of rope were stacked. He leaned against a barrel. "Nat Bowditch, eh? I've heard of you. Master Watson's brightest student you were." He shook his head dolefully. "And now you're becalmed. Just like I was at your age. Wouldn't think to look at me I was bright as a dollar once, would you? But I was. Wanted to make something of myself. But I didn't have a chance. Taken out of school, I was. Just like you. When I look at you, I can see myself as I was thirty — forty years ago. Becalmed, I was. Just like you."

Behind Nat a deep voice rumbled, "Avast there, Ben Meeker! Stow that gab about being becalmed!"

Nat looked around and saw keen blue eyes in a square ruddy face, under a shock of white hair.

Ben edged back. "I didn't say anything but the gospel truth, Sam Smith. This lad ought to be heading for college. But he's stuck fast in this chandlery for nine years. If he ain't becalmed — "

Sam said, "Bah! Only a weakling gives up when he's becalmed! A strong man sails by ash breeze!"

"A strong man, maybe, but what about a puny little — "

Sam gestured with his thumb over his shoulder. "Get out of here, and stay away from this boy. If I see you in here again, I'll give you a taste of a belaying pin!"

Ben scuttled out the door.

Sam put out his hand. "Nat Bowditch, aren't you? I know your father. He sailed under me more than once — before he had his own sloop."

Nat asked, "How do you 'sail by ash breeze'?"

Sam grinned. "When a ship is becalmed — the wind died down — she can't move — sometimes the sailors break out their oars. They'll row a boat ahead of the ship and tow her. Or they'll carry out anchors and heave them over, and the crew will lean on the capstan bars and drag the ship up to where the anchors are heaved over. Oars are made of ash — white ash. So — when you get ahead by your own get-up-and-get — that's when you sail by ash breeze'."

Nat straightened. "I like the sound of that."

"Of course you do." Sam nodded. "You're from a long line of seafaring men!" He lifted his voice to a bellow. "Mr. Hodges! I sent Ben packing! I'll show this lad around and it won't cost you a cent!"

Mr. Hodges called, "I can't ask you to do that, Sam."

"Who's asking me? I'm just doing it!" Sam grinned at Nat. "When an old fellow like me swallows the anchor, he's got to have something to do with his time!"

Mr. Hodges joined them. He gave a large, flat black notebook to Nat. "Would you like to write down everything Sam tells you?"

"Yes, sir! May I use the whole notebook?"

Mr. Hodges chuckled. "That and another one or two. When Sam starts talking, you'll fill a notebook in no time at all!"

Sam chuckled, too. "Come along, Nat. We'll start at the stern and work forward along the starboard bulkhead."

"Nat, do you know what he's talking about?" Mr. Hodges asked.

Nat squared his shoulders. "Yes, sir. The stern is the back and the starboard is the right and a bulkhead is a wall. We're starting at the back and working to the front along the right wall."

Sam clapped his hand on Nat's shoulder. "Make a sailor of him yet, if he ever grows to any size, won't we?" He picked up a flat piece of wood, shaped like a fourth of a pie. "First, Nat, I'll tell you about the log."

Nat studied the pie-shaped piece of wood. "That doesn't look much like a log to me."

"I'll tell you how it got its name. When a captain's at sea, he needs to know how far he has sailed in a day. To figure that out, he has to know how fast he is sailing and how long he has sailed that fast."

"That's arithmetic, isn't it? I like that!"

Sam nodded. "Nearly everything about navigation is arithmetic. Now, here's the way a sailor tells how fast he's going with a log. A long time ago, the Dutch sailors used to figure how fast they were going by throwing a piece of wood — they called it a log — overboard. One man stood forward in the bow of the ship and threw the log into the water. Another man stood aft, in the stern of the ship, and kept track of how many seconds it took until the stern of the ship passed the log.

"They knew how long the ship was. So when they knew how many seconds it took for the ship to go that many feet, they could figure out how many knots it was making. That was the way they measured their speed. They said they *logged* their speed because they figured it with a log. And that's why we call this pie-shaped piece of wood a *log;* because we use it to log the speed of the ship — you see?

"Now, here's the way we use this chip log. You see, it's weighted on the curved side, to make it stand on edge in the water. We heave it over the taffrail, so it trails along behind the ship. We have it tied to a reel of log line. As the ship moves forward, the log stands still in the water, and the line unwinds from the reel. Every so often there's a marker on the line. We call it a knot. As the reel unwinds, and the line goes over the taffrail of the ship, we begin to check the time when a special marker knot goes over."

Sam picked up a little glass, shaped like an hour glass, only much smaller. "We check the time with one of these little log glasses. This one is a twenty-eight-second glass. When the sand runs out, the sailor stops the log line. He counts how many knots have run out. That tells him how many knots his ship is going."

Nat squared his shoulders. "So now I know what it means to keep a log."

Sam bellowed, "No! That isn't keeping a log! Keeping a log is keeping the record of what happens on the voyage."

Nat said, "Then why don't they call it keeping the record?"

"Because one of the most important things in the record is the speed they have logged; so they call the whole record of what happens *the log.*"

Nat grinned. "I'm glad you're explaining things to me instead of Ben Meeker."

Sam said, "Ben won't be around here very soon again!"

Weeks passed. Nat had almost forgotten about Ben Meeker when he drifted into the chandlery again one day. Nat was busy at his desk behind the counter, writing things in his notebook.

Ben said, "What's that?"

"That," Nat told him, "is what I'm sailing by! That's an ash breeze!"

Ben shrugged. "I suppose you'll work that way at first. But nine years is a long time. You'll get mighty tired of sailing by ash breeze."

Ropes and Hodges Ship Chandlery

CHAPTER 7

THE ALMANAC

Before winter came again, Nat could find anything in the shop as quickly as Mr. Ropes or Mr. Hodges. But Sam still dropped in to talk. Sometimes Dr. Bentley dropped in, too.

Ben Meeker was lounging in the chandlery one day when Dr. Bentley stopped by. When the roly-poly minister had gone, Ben said, "Bright fellow. Powerful bright. Knew twenty languages when he was only twenty-five. No brighter than you'd have been, though, if you weren't becalmed."

The rest of that day, Nat found it hard to forget Ben Meeker.

Most of the time, though, he did not waste much time thinking of Ben's words. All day, he was too busy in the chandlery, or running errands. At night, he was too busy writing down everything he had learned that day.

One day an errand took him to a long building called a ropewalk. He watched the ropemakers walking backwards as they twisted the fibers into yarn, the yarn into strands, and the strands into rope. The ropemakers were proud of their work. "Most important thing on a ship," they said. "You can't sail a ship without cordage!"

That night Nat started a notebook on everything about rope.

Once an errand took him to a sail loft. He watched the sail makers cutting heavy canvas into strips and sewing it back together again. "Makes the sail stronger," they told him. "Most important thing on a ship — the sails. If it weren't for sails, how'd you get anywhere?"

Nat added more to his notebook; everything about sails.

Another errand took him to Ruck's Creek, called "Knocker's Hole," because all day you could hear the *thump, thump, thump* of the caulker's mallets, caulking the seams of ships. "Most important work on a ship," they told him. "If a ship isn't watertight, where'd you be?"

Nat added more notes — this time about caulking a ship. When Sam dropped in again, Nat showed him his new notebook. "Is there anything else to know about ships?"

Sam chuckled. "Lad, you haven't even begun! Navigation — that's something else again! Want to learn it? I reckon I could teach you."

So the winter Nat was thirteen, he started a new notebook: NAVIGATION Nathaniel Bowditch His Book.

By spring, the notebook was filled. Sam looked

through it one day. "It's all down there, lad. Get it in your head, and you'll have it!"

"What else can I learn?"

Sam shook his head and chuckled. "Blessed if I know! You've lightered all the cargo in my head!"

Mr. Ropes strolled back to Nat's desk. "Nat, run over to my house, and look up Surveying in the Chambers *Cyclopaedia*, will you? Hetty will show you where it is. Write down what it says about the start of surveying. You'll find everything you need on the desk."

Nat hurried over to Mr. Ropes' home. A cyclopaedia? What in the world was that? Well, Hetty would show him. . . .

Soon he was sitting at the desk in the library, with four big books in front of him: Ephraim Chambers' *Cyclopaedia, or Universal Dictionary of Arts and Sciences.* He turned the pages. Everything was here! Everything! I'd like to begin at A, he thought, and read right through to Z! But now he must find out about surveying.

The next thing Nat knew, Mr. Ropes was striding into the library, calling, "Nat! What in the name of sense happened to you? Did you go to sleep?"

"No, sir. I'm copying what it says about surveying. But there's a good bit to look up. It's a little hard to tell where the start of it is. I've looked up trigonometry — that's the kind of mathematics they use — and I've looked up theodolites — that's the kind of telescope they use. Then there's something about finding your position by sighting a star, so I got into astronomy. I can't tell yet where surveying starts — with astronomy, or trigonometry or the theodolite, or — "

"Nat Bowditch!" Mr. Ropes threw himself in a chair

and laughed until he wiped his eyes. "Where did it start? In what country? That's all I wanted to know! Give me that book a minute! . . . See? Right here! It says that surveying probably began in Egypt! So I was right!"

Nat said, "Oh . . . that's all you wanted to know?"

Mr. Ropes was still chuckling. "That was all. I'm sorry I put you to all that work for nothing."

Nat grinned. "It wasn't work. It was fun. May I keep the notes I made?"

"Of course. If you want to look up some more things in Chambers, help yourself any time. But" — he smiled — "after the chandlery closes, eh? Not in the middle of the afternoon." Mr. Ropes got up, still chuckling. "You'd better run along now. It's suppertime."

"What!" Nat jumped up and stared out the window. "Why — I — I've been here all afternoon!"

"You certainly have."

"I'm sorry. I'll finish up my work tonight."

Mr. Ropes said, "No need to do that."

But after supper Nat went back to the chandlery to finish the work he had not done. It was an unexpectedly warm night for early spring. He left the upper half of the Dutch door open.

He was busy at work when a voice called, "Nat?"

He looked up. Lizza was standing in the door. He smiled and hurried to let her in.

Lizza hesitated. "It's all right to stop a minute to talk to you? Mary always says we mustn't tag in here and bother you when you're busy."

"It's all right, Lizza."

They talked a while; then silence fell. "Funny — I

had so much to tell you," Lizza said. "Now I can't seem to think of it. . . . I miss you, Nat. I . . . I . . . When I go to tell you a joke and you're not there . . . I miss you most awfully." Suddenly Lizza wheeled and ran out the door. Nat knew she was crying.

His throat ached. "A good thing Hab taught me that boys don't blubber," he muttered. He went back to his work. After he'd finished his bookkeeping, he started a new notebook: THE PRACTICAL SURVEYOR: Nathaniel Bowditch. County of Essex and State of Massachusetts, New England. March the Seventh, 1787.

When Sam saw the new notebook, he said, "Now that's something I can help you with, too. Surveying's a lot like navigation — only it's a heap easier."

"You're sure it's easier?"

Sam chuckled. "Yes, sir! When you set up your theodolite good and level with your plumb line, the ground holds still. It won't heave and pitch like the deck of a ship when you're trying to shoot the sun. Yes, sir, surveying's lots easier. You'll get along fine with it."

Nat was still working on surveying when he got his first glimpse at an algebra book. That night, for the first time, he studied all night. The sky was paling in the east when he started another notebook: ALGEBRA AND MATHEMATICS: Nathaniel Bowditch His Book.

Every time he had a chance he borrowed the algebra book, to copy it into his notebook. Between times, he copied everything on mathematics he could find in the *Cyclopaedia*. Then he studied everything he could find on astronomy over again.

He was sixteen the summer he figured how to make an almanac. He felt a tingle go up his backbone. Just to think! A man could sit right here and figure out when the moon would rise every night next month — or next year — or ten years from now! He could figure out the way the sun would act; he could figure . . .

Ben Meeker shuffled into the chandlery one day. "What's that you're figuring on?"

"An almanac for the years from 1789 to 1823."

Ben sniffed. "Do tell. And what's your almanac going to have in it?"

"Just the regular things: the sun's rising, setting, declination, amplitude, place in the ecliptic — "

Ben stiffened. "You've no need to make fun of me!"

Nat stared. "But I'm not making fun. You asked me what is in my almanac, and I was telling you."

A strange voice said, "Pardon me — may I see your almanac?"

"Of course, sir." Nat handed his almanac to the stranger, and turned back to Ben. "It's just straight mathematics, Ben. You see — "

Ben threw up his hands. "Don't tell me! Save it for them as had a chance to go to school!" He shuffled out.

Nat turned to the stranger. "Something for you, sir?"

"Yes. A compass. Just a small one, please. For a child. We live in Cambridge. My little daughter says the streets get her mixed up."

Cambridge! Where Harvard was! Nat brought him the compass and gave him his change. At last the man looked up from the almanac.

"How old are you?"

"Sixteen, sir."

"But — but — this is amazing. You ought to be — Have you ever thought of going to Harvard?"

"I can't leave here, sir. I'm indentured."

The man frowned. "But that's — that's — " He stopped. He wrote on a slip of paper and gave it to Nat. "If anything happens that you can leave here — say within a year or two — write to me. I'd like a tutor for my children. I'm sure you could do that and go to Harvard, too. An almanac at sixteen!"

For weeks after that, Nat used to imagine the letter he'd write:

Dear Mr. Morris

I'm free now, and can come to Cambridge and be a Harvard man. The thing that freed me from my indenture was —

Nat's letter always stopped there. He couldn't think of anything that could happen to free him until he was twenty-one. And that was still five years away. Sometimes he agreed with Ben. Nine years was a long time to sail by ash breeze.

CHAPTER 8

"LOCK, STOCK, AND BOOKKEEPER"

One Thursday late in October Hab appeared in the door of the chandlery. "Ahoy the ship!" he yelled. Grinning, he entered with the rolling walk of a man who is used to a pitching deck under his feet. After he had shaken hands and slapped Nat on the back, he said, "What's all the excitement in town? Soldiers all over the place! Flags flying and drums beating! How'd you guess I'd get home just now?"

Nat laughed with him, then said, "President Washington's touring the country. He'll be here today."

"Washington!" Hab's eyes glowed. "Am I lucky! You know, Nat, when a man's at sea, he doesn't know what's going on at home. Every time you get home, you feel like you'd been asleep for six months. How's everyone?"

Nat gave him news of home. Mary was fine, Lizza was prettier than ever, William was getting along fine in navigation school, Sammy was bright, but he wouldn't study. Lois had knitted a pair of socks all by herself.

"And Father?" Hab asked.

Nat shook his head. Father wasn't doing so well. "Granny was right; when Mother died, Father lost his anchor to windward."

For a moment Hab's face was grim. He sighed and shook off his mood. "How soon can you close the shop? Then we'll go together and see them."

"I'll have to ask Mr. Hodges." Nat told him.

"What!" Then Hab must have remembered, too, the words of the indenture. Nat could not leave by day or by night without permission. "When a man's on shipboard, it's *Aye, aye, sir* and you obey on the double. But at least when I'm in home port I'm my own boss!"

Mr. Hodges came to shake hands with Hab. He said, "Nat, go along with Hab if you'd like. I'll close up. You needn't be back until tomorrow morning."

Nat thanked him. Hab and Nat left the shop together and walked down the street through the milling crowds. For a while they were silent. Then Hab remarked, "Mr. Hodges is mighty nice. But it's still like being in jail — being indentured!"

"I don't spend much time thinking about it," Nat said.

At one o'clock they joined the crowd that was forming on Court Street. The officers of the town were first, then the ministers, the merchants, the mechanics, and the schoolmasters with their students. They marched to the square near the entrance to Salem, and separated into two lines, leaving the roadway open between for the parade to pass. With a ruffle of drums and the shrilling of fifes the soldiers passed: the Salem Regiment in their red coats and light trousers, the soldiers from Ipswich in blue, the Independents in red, and the Artillery in black. It seemed to Nat every regiment looked smarter, stood straighter, and marched better than the last one.

At last someone shouted the news; they had hoisted the flag at Gardiner's Mills, two miles from town. That was the signal that Washington and his party were passing there. After a while — faintly at first and then louder — came the shrilling of fifes and rat-a-tat-tat of the drums. He was coming!

Nat heard the voice of Colonel Abbot, of the Salem Regiment: "Attention!"

The fifes and drums grew louder. The troops from Andover appeared in their dashing red uniforms, every button shining, leather gleaming. The cannon roared a salute that shook the town. The church bells clanged. Then a great shout went up. For there was President Washington — a tall, commanding man, riding horseback to enter the town. His coach and baggage wagon followed behind them.

Nat didn't realize how he had been yelling and cheering until the president had passed, and the troops had fallen in behind him.

Hab croaked, "I almost split my throat!"

Nat tried to answer and found he was croaking, too.

That night Nat spent with his family, watching the fireworks at the courthouse.

The next day, Washington and his party went on to Ipswich. Soon, Hab sailed again. Then Nat's days and nights settled down once more to the steady grind of sailing by ash breeze — working all day in the chandlery, studying late every night. He was reading straight through Chambers' *Cyclopaedia* now.

"There's a little bit about everything in it," he told Dr. Bentley, "but every time I read a short article on something, I wish I had a whole book. For instance, astronomy. I'd like a whole book about that."

Dr. Bentley said, "Isaac Newton's *Principia* is the book for you. That tells more about the stars than anything else. I have a copy. I'm going to Boston for a few days, but I'll try to send that over before I leave." And he hurried out of the chandlery.

That afternoon a youngster brought Nat the copy of *Principia*. Nat was too busy even to open the book then, but all day as he worked he kept smiling to himself. That evening he hurried through his supper, went up to his room, and lighted a candle. Smiling, he opened the book. A whole book about astronomy!

Disappointed, he stared at it. He couldn't read a word. He could figure out just enough to know that the book was written in Latin. Then another idea struck Nat — how long would it take to learn Latin, so he could read *Principia*? When Dr. Bentley got back Saturday, he'd ask him.

But Nat couldn't wait that long to ask someone. The next day he asked a Harvard graduate he knew how long it would take to learn Latin.

"Latin?" Elias Wilson said. "It's mighty hard. All the time I was in school, I had nightmares over Latin."

Nat showed him the copy of *Principia*. "How long would I have to study Latin to read this?"

Mr. Wilson threw up his hands. "Enough Latin to

read that? You'd need at least eight years, I'd say — under a good teacher!"

On Saturday Dr. Bentley dropped in at the chandlery. "Well, Nat, how are you enjoying *Principia?*"

"It's in Latin."

"Of course." Dr. Bentley smiled. "Latin is the language of scholars and scientists. Then they can all read each other's books. A very handy language, isn't it?"

"I suppose it is handy," Nat said, "if you know it. But I don't."

Dr. Bentley stared. "Dear me, I never thought of that!"

"I wondered if I could learn Latin . . ." Nat said.

"Of course! The very thing! Come see me this evening, Nat."

That evening Dr. Bentley said, "Here you are; a grammar, a dictionary and — by the way, do you know your Bible well?"

"Yes, sir, but it's in English."

Dr. Bentley chuckled. "It's in Latin, too, you know." He opened a New Testament in Latin. "Think of some passage you know well."

Nat repeated the opening verse of the Book of John: In the beginning was the Word, and the Word was with God, and the Word was God.

Dr. Bentley showed him the same passage in Latin: *In principio erat Sermo ille, et Sermo ille erat apud Deum, eratque ille Sermo Deus.*

Nat said, "I've figured out three words already: *In* is just the same as our word; *principio* is 'beginning': *Sermo* is 'word.' "

Dr. Bentley nodded. "*Sermo* — that's where we get our word 'sermon.'" He smiled. "Oh, you won't have any trouble with Latin. Latin isn't hard. It's *Principia* that will be hard. It's hard to understand even when you can read it!"

Back in his own room; Nat stared at the Latin books. Could he do it? Well, he could try! One thing, he thought, if he ever got a chance to go to Harvard, he'd need to know Latin. Just now a chance to go to Harvard seemed farther away than ever. But, he told himself, you never could tell what might happen. If the chance came, he'd be ready.

By the next summer, he had learned enough Latin to begin to translate *Principia*. It seemed to him that he lived in two worlds now. One was the world of the chandlery, where he kept books and sold marlinespikes, belaying pins, and hemp rope. The other was the world of the universe, where he translated Newton's *Principia* — a word at a time, until he had read another sentence. Sometimes he spent a whole evening on two or three sentences.

There was another world, too — the world of Salem. Every time Nat went on an errand he realized how Salem was growing. The men of Salem were proud of their town. Their "city," they called it now. Here it was — only 1790 — not even ten years since we'd won our independence — and Salem had doubled in size! Eight thousand people now! The people bragged of the growth of Salem, and of the daring of her sailors. Elias Hasket Derby's ships were going farther and farther from their home port. As Nat shouldered his way through the crowded wharves he heard talk of Russia and France and Spain, of Bombay and Calcutta.

One day he heard a chance remark that surprised him so much that he walked half a mile out of his way before he remembered where he was supposed to go.

"I hear Ropes and Hodges are selling the chandlery," a man remarked. "Samuel Ward is buying it."

"You sure?" the other man said.

"Well, I haven't seen the papers, but I heard . . . " The men moved out of earshot.

Nat walked on in a daze. Ropes and Hodges selling out! His heart pounded until the blood drummed in his ears. At last! His chance was coming. When Ropes and Hodges sold the chandlery, he'd be free! He'd get to go to Harvard after all. Seventeen wasn't too old. Mr. Morris had said, "If in a year or two something happens and you're free . . . " It had been just one year.

When Nat got back to the shop, Mr. Ropes was in the doorway. "You're back, Nat? Good. I've something to see about. I'll be gone about an hour. Then Jonathan and I have something to talk over with you." He smiled and was gone.

So it was true. Nat smiled, too. He went to his desk and started his letter to Mr. Morris:

. . . Since Ropes and Hodges are selling out, I'll be free of my indenture. I can come to Cambridge and tutor your children and study for Harvard. I've been study ing Latin for a year now, so . . .

Nat heard someone enter the shop. He laid down his

quill and stood. It was Samuel Ward — the man they said was buying the chandlery.

Mr. Ward smiled. "Don't bother about me, Nat. I just dropped in to look around. I don't know if you've heard it yet, but I'm buying the chandlery."

Nat grinned. "Congratulations, Mr. Ward. It's a fine chandlery."

Mr. Ward smiled, too. "And I'll get a fine bookkeeper with it, won't I? Yes, sir, I bought it — lock, stock, and bookkeeper."

Nat could feel the smile getting stiff on his face.

Mr. Ward didn't seem to notice. He chuckled at his own joke. "Lock, stock, and bookkeeper. That's pretty good, isn't it? Yes, Nat, I bought your indenture, right along with the cable and marline-spikes."

Nat forced himself to smile again. "That's right. I come with the rest of the supplies, don't I?" He picked up the letter to Mr. Morris and crushed it in his hand.

"What's that? Some figuring?" Mr. Ward asked. "I hear you're quite a hand with figures. I hope I didn't interrupt a problem — and mix you up."

"No," Nat told him, "you didn't interrupt anything. It was just a little problem. I know the answer now." He crushed the paper into a hard wad and tossed it into the waste basket.

Yes, he knew the answer. The answer was — no freedom until he was twenty-one. Four more years in the chandlery. Then it would be too late for Harvard. He'd still have to sail by ash breeze.

CHAPTER 9

ANCHOR TO WINDWARD

When it was time to close the chandlery for the night, Mr. Ropes and Mr. Hodges still had not returned. Nat closed the shop and went to supper, then climbed the stairs to his room. As he entered, a sudden thought struck him. Soon this wouldn't be his room. He'd go to live in Mr. Ward's house. Nat looked around the room that had been his home for five years. Suddenly his stomach felt hollow.

Someone rapped on the door; Mr. Hodges entered. "I saw Sam Ward," he said. "He told me he'd been in and talked to you."

"Yes, Mr. Hodges." Nat made himself smile again. "He said he'd bought you out — lock, stock, and bookkeeper."

Mr. Hodges smiled briefly. "There's one thing, Nat — I suggested to Mr. Ward that you go on living here — if it's all right with you."

"Not leave this room?"

"Unless you want to."

Nat turned quickly to the window and stared hard at the ships in the harbor. After a while he said, "That suits me fine. I've always liked this view."

Mr. Hodges said, "Good! We like having you here!"

It was July, and the summer doldrums had settled over the chandlery. Nat was deep in his Latin when Lizza's voice called from the door, "May I come in?"

"Of course, Lizza!" Nat got up quickly and went to meet her, grinning. "You know what? Every year since you were eight, you've gotten twice as pretty as you were the year before."

"Hmmm . . . " Lizza bit her tongue and rolled her eyes. "I'm nineteen now . . . eight from nineteen . . . " She sighed. "You mathematician! I wish you could at least pay a compliment without arithmetic! Eight from nineteen is eleven. Twice as pretty every year . . . Goodness, I'm twenty-two times as pretty!"

Nat laughed. "You're two thousand and forty-eight times as pretty. Keep count on your fingers as I double one eleven times: two — four — eight — sixteen — thirty-two — sixty-four — one hundred twenty-eight — two hundred fifty-six — five hundred twelve — one thousand and twenty-four — and two thousand and forty-eight!"

"And next year . . . " Lizza said.

"Four thousand and ninety-six times as pretty! And now tell me — what's making that frown between your eyebrows?"

"I'm worried about David Martin and Mary. Did you know David wants to marry her?"

Nat blinked. "But don't you like David?"

"Of course! He's grand! But Mary says she won't marry a sailing man!" Lizza's eyes flashed. "Can you imagine that? Five generations of sea captains in her blood, and she won't marry a sailor!"

"Maybe that's why she feels that way," Nat said. "Remember what you told me once? Sometimes women get a little upset about the sea. Or maybe Mary saw that item in the paper about Marblehead. It's a sailing town, too — with about 6000 people; and 459 widows and 865 orphans."

Lizza nodded. "I think that's what upset her. She just feels she can't marry a sailor and spend most of her life wondering where he is, how he is, and if he'll ever get home safely again. But, Nat, she *loves* David."

"You want me to talk to Mary?"

"Please," Lizza urged. "She'll listen to you. She says you have the brains of the family — you and William. Of course . . . "

Nat grinned. "It's just about mathematics? That's all right, I'll explain it to her mathematically — you know — two plus two — and things like that."

That evening Nat went to see Mary. He didn't beat around the bush. "I heard that David Martin wants to marry you?"

Mary looked up quickly from the hank of yarn she was winding into a ball. "What did he say to you?"

"Nothing. How do you feel about marrying a sailor?"
Mary said, "I won't."

"Good enough," Nat said. "I'll see that David stops bothering you. After all, there are plenty of other girls. I think Hester Githens would marry David in a minute.

I'll mention her to David — get him interested — "

"Nat Bowditch! Don't you dare tell David — "

"No trouble at all," Nat said. "That's what brothers are for — to take care of their sisters. I'll see David tomorrow. I'll talk about Hester — get him interested. In no time at all, he'll fall in love and marry her. Then, the next time he goes to sea, you won't have to worry about what happens to him."

Mary jumped up, spilling her yarn. Her eyes snapped the way Granny's used to, but dimples were fighting to show around her mouth. "Nat Bowditch! You get out of here before I throw something!"

Nat grinned. "I'm not afraid. I was just going anyway."

The night after Mr. and Mrs. David Martin moved into their little home, their friends gathered for a housewarming. Nat got there late. He poked his head in the door.

"Do I dare come in?"

Mary ran to meet him with a hug and a kiss. "Always! I don't know why, but David seems to think you're quite a man! He said if I ever had trouble with you, I'd swing from a yardarm!"

Nat laughed and went to find Lizza. Lizza was in the corner, telling a story to a girl of ten or eleven — a youngster with a mop of black curls and a face that seemed all violet eyes. Nat recognized her; she was Captain Boardman's little daughter, Elizabeth. He smiled at them. "The two Elizabeths!"

The youngster's eyes sparkled. "We do have the same name, don't we? Only I wish someone had nicknamed me 'Lizza,' too. How did Lizza ever get that name?"

Lizza said, "I think Nat called me that when he was too little to talk plain."

Elizabeth studied Nat gravely. "Funny to think you were young once, isn't it? I suppose you seem older because of your brains. People say figures just run out of your ears. But I don't see any." Then, in a swift change of mood, she said, "Mary will be awfully happy here, won't she? I mean — she knows how to be happy. Being happy takes a lot of practice, don't you think?"

Lizza said, "Go tell David that, Elizabeth. He'll love it."

When Elizabeth had gone, Nat whistled softly. "How do you keep up with her?"

Lizza smiled. "She's a dear child. But she does say the oddest things. Sometimes I think she must have been born knowing them. I tell her she has eyes in the back of her heart."

Nat smiled. "And *she* says odd things? I think you're quite a pair."

When Nat got back to his room that night it seemed emptier and more lonely than it had at any time since his first night there, five years ago. He sat down and tried to study, but the words meant nothing. He went to the window and watched the moon follow her path through the stars. Some day, when he had translated all of Newton, he'd know more about why the moon followed that certain path through the heavens.

He remembered his mother's words: "I made a sort of saying for myself, Nat: *I will lift up my eyes unto the stars. . . .*"

Finally Nat turned and went back to his work.

The months passed, and winter came again. One day the Reverend Dr. Prince dropped in at the chandlery and asked, "How's Newton coming along, Nat?"

"I think I'll make quite a career of Newton," Nat told him. "At the rate I'm going, it will take me about ten years to read *Principia*. First, I have to figure out what it means in English, and then I have to figure out what it *means*."

Dr. Prince shook his head. "Why you keep at it I'll never know. But it will go faster after a while, Nat."

A year later, one raw December day, Dr. Prince was in the chandlery again. "How's Newton coming now?"

"Better!" Nat told him. "I think it's only going to take me five years now."

Dr. Prince shook his head again.

Elizabeth Boardman came into the chandlery, her eyes sparkling. "Here's a note for you, from Lizza, Nat. I'm to wait for an answer, please."

Nat excused himself and read the note. Lizza and Mary were planning a party to surprise David — the ninth of December. Could Nat be there, sure? Nat smiled at the postscript: "Shhh! It's a secret! Tear this note across eleven times and scatter the 2048 pieces to the wind!"

Nat said, "Tell Lizza the answer is *yes*. I'll be there."

Dr. Prince smiled at the youngster. "Elizabeth, maybe you can figure this out for me. Why do you think Nat reads Latin?"

Elizabeth rolled her eyes gravely from one to the other. "It's his brain, don't you think? I mean — it's awfully restless. He probably reads Latin to keep it quiet. The way girls stitch samplers, you know."

Dr. Prince blinked. When Elizabeth had gone, he started out, too, still shaking his head. He turned back, "I'm even forgetting why I came. Can you see me tonight, Nat, after you close? I've something to show you."

When Nat reached Dr. Prince's home that night, he was waiting in his study. "I don't know whether you've ever heard of it, Nat, but we have a special library here — The Salem Philosophical Library. A group of us started it about ten years ago. We've been adding to it, year after year. Now, I think we have the best scientific library between here and Philadelphia. You may never have heard of it — since it's a private library. Only members can use it."

"How much does it cost to be a member, sir?"

Dr. Prince said, "About fifty pounds."

Nat's hopes sank. Years yet before he'd be free. And even then he'd have nothing.

"I've been talking to the members, Nat. We have decided to make an exception in your case; you're to be allowed to read the books. If you'd like to . . . Would you like to, Nat?"

Nat struggled to swallow the lump in his throat. "Yes, sir. More than anything in the world."

"Good!" Dr. Prince nodded toward the shelves. "Help yourself." He turned to the papers on his desk and began working.

Nat opened one of the books and read the name on the flyleaf. He asked, "This Richard Kirwan — is he a member of the library?"

Dr. Prince looked up from his work. "Kirwan? No, he's a great Irish scientist. We started this collection with one hundred and sixteen books from his private library.

That was during the war. The books were part of the cargo of a prize ship — the *Mars*. She struck her colors to a privateer of ours — the *Pilgrim*. Some day I'll tell you the story." He bent over his work again.

Nat stared at the book, smiling. The *Pilgrim!* These were the books captured on the *Mars* and auctioned off to Dr. Stearns! He chose a book, wrote the name of it on the pad of paper, thanked Dr. Prince again, and went back to his room. Before he started reading, he wrote a note:

> Notice to Lizza:
>   Be it known by these presents that on this day Nathaniel Bowditch started collecting his expectations on the *Pilgrim*. He's having a chance to read the "finest scientific library between here and Philadelphia." P.S. Shhh! This is secret! Tear this note across twelve times and scatter the four thousand and ninety-six pieces to the wind! N.B.

He grinned as he folded the note. When he saw Lizza at the party, he'd give it to her. He put it in his coat pocket so he would not forget it.

From downstairs came faint sounds of confusion. Then feet thudded on the steps and David Martin called, "Nat! Nat!"

Nat jerked the door open.

David stood a moment panting and then spoke in gasps. "Lizza . . . she fell on the stairs . . . it's pretty bad . . . the doctor says . . . you'd better come!"

That night, and the days and nights that followed, were a nightmare of fighting to save Lizza. Nat was by her, holding her hand, when she died.

The night after the funeral Nat walked alone out on the wharf. He shivered, thrust his hands in his pockets, and found the note he'd written Lizza. Slowly he tore it to bits and scattered the pieces on the water. He watched the ebbing tide carry them out until they sank. He thought of Tom Perry and the note they'd scattered on the water in his memory. He could almost hear Lizza's whisper again: "If you squinch your eyes, Nat, it looks exactly like flowers — almost — doesn't it?"

Nat clenched his hands and stared at the water until it blurred. He looked up at the sky. The stars blurred, too. "I don't see any help in the stars! Not now!"

Behind him, someone spoke. "Nat?"

Nat wheeled and saw David. He snapped, "What do you want?"

"Mary sent me. She was worried."

Nat spoke harshly. "She needn't worry. Tell her I've gone home to read Latin. It's good for restless brains — keeps them quiet, like stitching samplers." He shoved past David and left the wharf.

David fell in step beside him. Silent, they walked out toward the Beverly Ferry — then turned and tramped back across town toward Gallows Hill. There was no sound but the crunch of their feet in the snow.

At last Nat turned toward Hodges' house. When they got there, he held out his hand. "I'm sorry, David. Give Mary my love. Good night."

David said, "I'll tell her about the Latin. It sounds like a good anchor to windward. People that can use their brains are lucky. You'll never abandon ship, Nat."

In his room, Nat opened the Kirwan book again. He

tried to read, but the words made no sense. He opened a new notebook and began to copy an article, a word at a time, saying each word aloud as he wrote it.

When dawn came, he was writing swiftly, filling page after page with his fine scrawl. When he realized it was light, he took off his clothes, washed, dressed again, and went to the chandlery.

He was busy with the bellows, trying to coax the embers of the fire into flame, when the door opened and a gust of wind whipped through the shop.

Without looking up he snapped, "Shut the door, can't you?"

"I'm trying!" a girl's voice gasped.

Nat jumped to his feet and turned. Elizabeth Boardman was struggling to close the door.

Nat flinched. If she mentions Lizza's name, he told himself, I'll bite her head off, and then she'll bawl . . . He groaned and hurried to close the door.

"Thank you, Nat!" Elizabeth sighed and brushed back a curl with a dust-begrimed hand.

Nat looked at her grimy hands, her soot-streaked face. "Where in the world have you been? And what are you doing out this time of morning?"

"I brought you something." She handed him a packet, carefully wrapped in white paper — with her grimy fingerprints on it. "I'm sorry it's dusty. It was in the storeroom. Will you open the door, please, and shut it after me? I have to get home before anyone wakes up and misses me."

Before Nat could collect his wits, she was gone.

He unwrapped the package. It was a book — in Latin.

CHAPTER 10

FREEDOM

Later that same morning a boy brought Nat a note from Nathan Read, who had opened an apothecary shop in Salem.

Dear Nat

I have an apprentice in my shop who's interested in scientific things, too. If you'd like to come around on Sunday evening and talk with us, we'll enjoy having you.

Yours sincerely

NATHAN READ

During the rest of the week, Nat looked forward to Sunday evening. Mr. Read certainly would be an interesting man to know better. He was a jack of all trades who was a master of them, too.

Nat had heard stories of Mr. Read's days at Harvard — how when Nathan Read was just an undergraduate, studying Hebrew, the professor in charge of the class got sick, and young Nathan had taken over the class and taught it.

He'd graduated with honors, had come to Salem and studied medicine; then he had decided to open his apothecary shop. Besides all his interest in medicine and drugs, he liked to work with machinery. He had applied to Congress for a patent on a steam engine he'd made to run a boat. He had also tried to get Congress to give him a patent on his idea for a steam wagon, too. But the Congressmen said that that idea was so crazy they wouldn't even consider it.

On Sunday evening, Mr. Read showed Nat his workbench, his tools, and his books. "You're welcome to use anything here," he said. He opened one heavy, leatherbound book. "This is one of the best things I have, but it's in French. Do you know French?"

"Not yet," Nat told him, "but I could learn it." And he told Mr. Read how he was studying Latin.

Mr. Read said, "A good idea! A grammar, a New Testament, and a dictionary, eh? I can let you have those in French."

Late the next afternoon, when Nat had a few minutes of free time in the chandlery, he opened the New Testament in French. He repeated the opening words of the Book of John to himself in English: In the beginning was the Word, and the Word was with God, and the Word was God.

Then he read them in French: *Au commencement était la Parole, et la Parole était avec Dieu, et la Parole était Dieu.*

Frederic Jordy came in the shop. "I hear you want to study French, Mr. Bowditch? Maybe we could trade lessons. You could help me with my English, and I'll help you with French." He saw the New Testament. "You're beginning already, eh?"

"I've just looked at the first sentence," Nat said. "But I already see two words that are just the same as in English: *commencement* and — "

Mr. Jordy clutched his head. "No, no, that isn't the way to pronounce it!"

"Why not? It's the way it's spelled."

"But you must learn to pronounce it in French. Like this!" And Mr. Jordy gave the word its French sound.

Nat said, "I don't see how you get that out of it. French pronunciation must be crazy."

"Not at all!" Mr. Jordy insisted. "It is English pronunciation that is crazy. Take three words: rough, cough, and dough. Excepting for their first letter, they are all spelled alike. But how are they pronounced?"

Nat smiled. "All right; English pronunciation is crazy. But all I want of French is to be able to read it. Can you help me with that — and not bother about the pronunciation?"

"Never! I couldn't stand hearing you mangle it!"

Nat shrugged. "All right; I'll learn to pronounce it, too."

With Latin and *Principia,* with French and the Kirwan books, and his evenings with Mr. Read, Nat filled every minute when he wasn't working at the chandlery, eating, or sleeping.

December passed; a new year began. A nor'easter

howled in from the Atlantic and smothered Salem in snowdrifts. For three days Nat sat in the chandlery and studied almost undisturbed.

The fourth morning Elizabeth Boardman came.

Nat smiled at her. "My first customer today. What can I do for you?"

"When Father gets back from the West Indies, I want to surprise him."

Nat smiled. "That shouldn't be hard to do. You can surprise anyone without half trying."

Elizabeth studied him gravely. "Sometimes I'm not sure what you're talking about."

"We're even," Nat told her. "How do you want to surprise your father?"

"With a present. He always brings me something." Elizabeth's eyes danced. "This time I want to give him a present. Something he can use."

"Hmmm. How much can you pay for it?"

"Oh, that doesn't matter. Mother said I could get anything I wanted to."

Nat studied. "Parallel rulers might be nice."

"Do you suppose Father has them already?"

Nat exploded. "Of course! What sort of sailing master do you think he is?" Then he apologized quickly. "I'm sorry. I didn't mean to bark at you."

"I know. I'm just like a chair you stumble over in the dark," Elizabeth said. "It isn't the chair's fault, but you kick it anyhow."

Nat blinked. "What are you talking about?"

"Your brain. It's too fast. So you stumble on other people's dumbness. And — you want to kick something."

Nat felt his face get hot. "But I shouldn't."

Elizabeth agreed. "No, you shouldn't, because even if people are dumb, they aren't chairs, are they? They do have feelings."

"Lizza was right," Nat said. "You do have eyes in the back of your heart. Come on over here, and I'll show you how your father uses parallel rulers." He smiled. "And you may ask all the questions you want to, and I promise not to bark."

In the weeks that followed, he explained a lot of things to Elizabeth; sextants and logs, spyglasses and dividers. It was March before she finally decided on the present — binoculars.

When she had paid for them she said, "I'm going to watch for his ship tomorrow — up on the captain's walk on the roof of our house."

Nat stared. "Tomorrow? Why are you so sure he'll come tomorrow?"

Elizabeth flushed, fingering the screw on the binoculars. "I didn't mean just tomorrow; I mean — I'm going to watch for him every morning — until he comes." And she hurried out.

Smiling, Nat watched her go. That hadn't been what she meant, at all. She was going to watch for her father's ship tomorrow morning.

And I wouldn't be surprised, Nat told himself, if Captain Boardman's ship did arrive tomorrow.

The next morning Dr. Bentley stopped at the chandlery with news. Dr. Bentley often brought the first news of a returning ship. Almost every morning he took a walk out on the Neck and stared out over the water.

Captain George Crowninshield had built a lookout there for him on a high point — a solid granite base, with steps leading up to a seat. There was a flagstaff there, so that Dr. Bentley could run up signals.

"There's bad news, Nat. A ship's coming in with its flag at half-mast. Something's happened to the captain."

Nat's tongue felt thick in his mouth. "What ship?"

Dr. Bentley shook his head. "I'm not sure. I ran my signal to half-mast, and then hurried back. I want to be at the wharf when the ship anchors."

I know who it is, Nat thought. He felt a chill prickle his scalp and run down his spine.

It was Sam who brought the final news. Captain Boardman had died in the West Indies.

Two other ships anchored in Salem Harbor that day. Men crowded the chandlery with talk and with orders. It was late that night before Nat locked the door.

He hadn't thought where he was going until he found himself crossing the Commons toward Captain Boardman's big white house. As he neared the house, he looked up toward the captain's walk and saw Elizabeth.

When he reached the house, old Minna, Mrs. Boardman's maid, opened the door.

Nat said, "I don't want to disturb Mrs. Boardman. I just wanted to speak to Elizabeth. I believe she's on the captain's walk."

Old Minna dabbed at her eyes with her apron. "Oh, Mr. Nat, if only you will! The child is bound and determined to be up there. I can't do a thing with her. I don't dare tell her mother. I swore Elizabeth was in bed, fast asleep."

Nat climbed to the captain's walk. The trap door creaked when he opened it.

Elizabeth whirled to face him. "I won't come down! I . . . Oh, it's you, Nat. I'm glad." She clutched the binoculars. "Mother says I may keep them."

"That's good," Nat said. "But we don't need them for what we're going to see now. I'm going to show you how to tell time by the Big Dipper and the North Star. Can you find the Dipper?"

Elizabeth studied the stars a moment. "Is that it — upside down?"

"You've found it, all right. Now, look at the stars on the side of the Dipper across from the handle. And imagine a line running through them and slanting down."

"It goes through another star."

Nat said, "That's the North Star. If you think of the North Star as the middle of your clock face, and the line from it through those other stars as the hour hand, you can tell time."

"It says about one o'clock. Is that right?"

"No, this clock runs backwards."

"Is it eleven o'clock?"

"No, there's one other difference. It takes twenty-four hours for the Big Dipper to swing around the North Star. So every hour space on the clock face stands for two hours."

Elizabeth sighed. "There goes your brain again." She studied. "Ten o'clock?"

"You're doing fine." Nat went on talking.

Finally Elizabeth said, "I'm sleepy, Nat."

They tiptoed down from the captain's walk. Old Minna was waiting for them. She went to the door with Nat.

"Bless you, Mr. Nat. I don't know what you said to her, but there's peace in her eyes now."

"We looked at the stars," Nat told her. "Sometimes, if you look at the stars long enough, they sort of shrink your troubles down to size."

Minna shook her gray head. "I haven't a notion what you're talking about, but I'm sure it's wonderful. You know, you're real humanlike — in spite of your brains."

Nat bit back a smile. "Thank you, Minna."

"You're indentured, aren't you, Mr. Nat?"

"Yes, Minna."

"Have you thought about what you'll do when you're free?"

Nat smiled. "First thing, I'll hire a fife and drum and have a one-man parade down Derby Street!"

A puzzled frown wrinkled Minna's forehead. "I've never seen a body do that. My brother John was indentured. I remember what he said when he was free. He said he felt real lost-like at first."

Sometimes, in the two years that followed, Nat thought of Minna's words. What would he do when he was free? Where would he find a place in the world? He thought about it especially whenever Hab or William or David was home between voyages. Each of them talked of "his ship." Each had found his place in the world.

Nat wondered again, when the last of his brothers went to sea. Sammy was sixteen when he swaggered into the chandlery one day and grinned down at Nat. "Just came to say good-by for a while. My ship's bound for Jamaica."

Nat smiled and shook hands and watched Sammy swagger out of the shop to board his ship. His ship. Sammy had found his place, too. Nat shrugged and turned back to his bookkeeping. Even while he was still thinking of Sammy, his glance flicked down a column of figures and his fingers jotted the answer. He realized his mind was wandering. He jerked his thoughts back in line, and added the figures again. He'd been right the first time. For almost nine years now, he'd been right about figures. What would he do with the next nine years? Go on adding columns and columns of figures?

The week before he was twenty-one Nat wakened with a feeling of something hanging over him. He sat up slowly and looked about his garret room. How many times, his first year in this room, had he fought back tears? He had been so alone. No one to say good night to, no one to sit and talk to — no one. He had had nothing but the books he studied and the things he copied into his notebooks.

For nine years this room had been his home. In a week, it would all be over. He'd be free. He could come and go as he pleased.

"I'll be free," he muttered, "and I know now what Minna's brother meant. I'm beginning to feel lost-like, too."

As he got out of bed a piece of white paper under the door caught his glance. He picked it up and read:

Dear Nat

In case you've forgotten, you have just another week until your twenty-first birthday. We hope you'll want to stay on in this room. We're sure it would feel empty without you. So, as long as you care to stay, and whatever you're doing, think of this room as your home. will you? We . . .

There was more, but the words blurred.

CHAPTER 11

WHAT NEXT?

On Tuesday of Nat's last week at the chandlery Ben Meeker drifted in and leaned against a barrel. "Well, Nat, it's almost over — seems like — eh?"

"What do you mean — *seems like?*" Nat asked him.

"I told you nine years ago you were becalmed, didn't I? And you are. Your indenture's almost over — but what can you do? Keep on working in a chandlery, like as not." Ben shook his head. "And if things keep going from bad to worse, you won't have this job very long. Our merchant ships will be wiped off the seas."

Nat snorted. "Bosh!" But he knew there was something in what Ben said. American ships were having a hard time. Ever since America had won her freedom from England, she had to fight for her rights on the high seas. Now England and France were at war, and things were in a worse fix than ever. President Washington was trying to keep America at peace with both countries. He had declared his country's neutrality — had said America would not side with either country. Now both England and France were attacking American ships. Yes, there was something in what Ben said.

Ben sighed and shook his head again. "We ought to have sided with France back in '89 when their revolution started. If we had, we wouldn't be having trouble with France now. They'd be helping us against England."

Nat said, "Humph! The French people killed their king. Now they've got Napoleon. He doesn't sound much better than a king to me."

"We should have sided with France," Ben repeated. He pulled a dirty scrap of paper from his pocket. "I got a piece here that I cut out of a newspaper. The editor put it just right. He gives Washington a good going-over for not siding with France." He unfolded the paper. "Listen to this!"

"No! I don't want to hear it!" Nat said. "And I don't think editors have any right to talk against the President. Americans ought to stand together!"

Behind Nat someone chuckled. Nat turned. Dr. Bentley was looking at him with a twinkle. "Is this a political argument?"

Nat shrugged. "No argument at all. Ben's got an article there that talks against the President. I said I didn't want to hear it. I said that sort of thing ought to be stopped."

To Nat's amazement, Dr. Bentley shook his head. "No, Nat. We can't have freedom — unless we have freedom."

Nat stiffened. "Does that mean the right to tell lies?"

Dr. Bentley smiled. "It means the right to have our

own opinions. Human problems aren't like mathematics, Nat. Every problem doesn't have just one answer; sometimes you get several answers — and you don't know which is the right one."

Nat felt his face get hot. "But people don't have a right to talk against the President, do they? That's going too far!"

"Years ago," Dr. Bentley said, "before we won our independence, the *Essex Almanac* published something about freedom of the press. It was true then; it's just as true now. I may not have the exact words, but it went something like this:

"The Press is dangerous in a despotic government, but in a free country it is very useful, *so long as it is free;* for it is very important that people should be told everything that concerns them. If we argue against any branch of liberty, just because sometimes people abuse that liberty, then we argue against liberty itself. *In a free country, the press must be free.*"

Ben waved his dirty scrap of paper. "See? Dr. Bentley agrees with this! See?"

Dr. Bentley shook his head. "No. I just agree with a man's right to say what he thinks."

Ben mumbled something and shuffled out of the chandlery.

"Well, Nat?" Dr. Bentley said.

"I never thought of it that way," Nat admitted, "but I guess that's the way it has to be; 'we can't have freedom unless we have freedom.' And that means freedom to speak our minds."

Dr. Bentley nodded soberly. "Remember that, always." Then his eyes twinkled. "Why did Ben come around this morning? To shake his head over your prospects?"

Nat grinned. "That was about it. Ben certainly enjoys groaning about hard times, doesn't he?"

"Well, Nat, I don't know what next year or the year after holds for you. But I've an offer for you right now. Captain Gibaut and I are going to do a survey of Salem. There's a place for you on our crew. It's nothing permanent — but it's a job for a few months — if you'd like."

"I'd like that fine — and thank you for thinking of me."

"I'm doing us a favor," Dr. Bentley told him. "We can use your knack with figures."

That evening Nat went over to tell Mary the news.

Mary smiled, then sighed. "I'm glad you're not going to sea, Nat. We have enough men at sea. I wonder where they all are tonight — Hab and William and Sammy — and David?"

"They're all right, Mary."

"You don't know what it's like for a woman, Nat," Mary went on. "You say good-by to your man. His ship stands out from Salem Harbor. Then the months pass — sometimes the years — with no word from him."

"They'll be coming back; just wait and see."

"I do wait," Mary told him. "I spend most of my life waiting."

Nat could not think of an answer to that.

It was less than a month later that Sammy's ship returned from Jamaica — without Sammy. He had died of fever in the West Indies.

Nat took the word to Mary.

She stared at him with stricken eyes. "I wonder who'll be next?"

Again Nat could think of no answer. He wished he could tell her that all the others were safe. But he wasn't so sure. Every day, as he worked on the survey of Salem, he heard more stories of trouble at sea. It seemed that every ship that returned brought bad news.

Captain Ware came home, raging because the English had searched his ship and had taken two of his men. "Swore they'd deserted from the English navy! Humph! Neither lad had been off soundings till he sailed with me."

Captain Reed came home, grim-faced. He'd had a running fight with a French privateer and had lost three men. "Shot down in cold blood, they were! What's Congress going to do to protect our shipping? Just sit there in Philadelphia and talk about it?"

Someone said John Jay was in England, trying to iron out our problems with the British.

Captain Gibaut snorted at that. "Bah! Diplomats can't settle this! We need a navy! I'm lucky to be surveying Salem instead of walking a quarter-deck!"

In November, John Jay returned, bringing the treaty he had worked out with England. Captain Gibaut roared at the terms of the treaty. "You call that a 'matter-of-give-and-take'? Bah! We give and England takes! And not a word about that business of the British searching our ships and seizing our men! That Jay treaty hasn't settled anything! As long as England thinks she rules the seas, we're going to have trouble with her! If I had the sense of a cabin boy, I'd never go to sea again!"

Two days later, Gibaut had signed on to command a

Derby ship, as soon as the survey was finished. He was to take the *Henry* on a voyage around the Cape of Good Hope to the Isle of Bourbon, off the east coast of Africa.

One day he said, "Nat, have you ever thought of going to sea?"

Nat remembered all the brawny swaggering seamen who had crowded the chandlery. He thought of stories of captains who could knock a man from starboard rail to larboard scuppers with one blow of a fist. "I'm five-feet-five when I stretch," he said. "Do you think I have the build for a life at sea?"

Gibaut chuckled. "You wouldn't throw much weight on a halyard — that's one thing sure. But you'd do all right as ship's clerk. You might work up to supercargo."

"What's the difference," Nat asked, "between clerk and supercargo?"

Gibaut shrugged. "The pay, mostly. They both do the figuring. It's an easy job — if you have a head for figures. In port, there's plenty to do. We may sell one cargo, buy another, sell that in the next port, and buy a third. But between ports, you'd have an easy time. No watches to stand, no decks to swab."

"I wonder," Nat said, "if a captain would let me take my notebooks on board and study between ports?"

Gibaut stared. "Are you still studying? What else do you want to know? Dr. Bentley says you already know more mathematics than any man in the country!" He shrugged. "But, if you still want to study, you could bring your notebooks along for all of me!"

Nat's heart jumped. Was Gibaut talking about his going on the *Henry?* In a Derby ship? Nat's scalp tingled, just thinking about the Derby ships: the *Quero,* that took the news of Lexington to London; the *Astrea*, that brought the news of the peace from Paris; the *Lighthouse* — first ship to carry the stars and stripes to the Baltic; the *Grand Turk* — first New England ship in the Orient.

He looked at Gibaut. "You — you're talking about my sailing with you?"

Gibaut roared, "What in blazes did you think I was talking about?" He chuckled again. "That's it, Nat. A berth as clerk on the *Henry*. And you'll be allowed cargo space for a venture of your own — something you want to take along to sell."

"How much room could I have?" Nat asked.

Gibaut shrugged. "Any reasonable amount."

"When I finish my work on the survey," Nat said, "I'll have a hundred and thirty-five dollars. Could I invest that much in a venture, and have room for it?"

"A hundred and . . . " Gibaut shouted with laughter. "Don't worry, Nat. There'll be plenty of room for your venture."

"I wonder," Nat said, "why they call it a *venture?*"

Gibaut was still chuckling. "Because it is a venture — a risk. Any cargo is a risk. When we get to Bourbon, we may find people begging for our cargo and we may sell everything for three times what we paid for it. Or maybe when we get there, they won't want anything we have. Maybe we'll find there have been eight or ten ships there just ahead of us. Then we'll lose our shirts. We never know."

"I wouldn't want to lose my whole hundred and thirty-five dollars. I wonder if there's anything I could be sure I'd sell?"

"You can't be sure of anything," Gibaut said. "But ask

Monsieur Bonnefoy about it. He ought to know. He comes from Bourbon. Fact is, he's going home on the *Henry*."

The next day Nat questioned Monsieur Bonnefoy.

"A venture to Bourbon, monsieur?" Bonnefoy said. "Take something in the line of clothing. You see, Bourbon produces almost nothing but coffee and sugar. We've always depended on our mother country for everything. Since the beginning of the Revolution, though, France has been too busy with battles to keep up with our needs. Too much bloodshed — not enough boots and shoes."

"Boots and shoes?" Nat said. "I think I can get shoes reasonably . . ."

Soon he had invested almost all his money in boots, half boots, and shoes, and had ordered them to be packed for the journey to Bourbon.

He got out his notebook on navigation and studied it all over again. He borrowed a logbook from Captain Gibaut, and copied it — just to be sure he knew how a log was kept.

David Martin's ship anchored. He sympathized with Mary over Sammy's death, but he said, "Don't blame the sea, dear. Men die of yellow fever in the States, too. Remember how it was with Philadelphia in '93?" And his eyes lighted at the news that Nat was going to sea. He gave Nat a sextant. "You'll catch on to using it in no time," he said.

"I've tried them out — on land of course. I guess at sea . . ." Nat paused.

David chuckled. "First time you try to shoot the sun, it's about like trying to thread a needle when you're running downhill."

Nat told David about his venture, and the logbook he'd made. "The only thing I'm trying to decide is — which notebooks to take with me."

David smiled and shook his head. "Still studying? Take all of them, why don't you?"

"I wouldn't want anything to happen to them. I mean — if the *Henry* . . ."

David chuckled. "If the *Henry* sinks, where'll you be?"

Mary gasped. *"David!"*

"But what if I happened to be saved and the notebooks — " Nat asked. "I tell you, David, there's a lot of information in them."

David chuckled again. "Make a bargain with Gibaut — if anything happens to the *Henry,* you want to go down with your ship."

"David Martin!" Mary gasped, and then she smiled. "You!"

Nat smiled, too, and told them good night.

Back in his room, he took the sextant out of its case. He stood, feet apart, swaying with the imaginary movement of the deck, and lifted the sextant. Some day soon, on the *Henry* . . .

The next day he was down at the wharf, watching the loading of the *Henry,* when he saw Captain Gibaut striding toward him. Gibaut certainly seemed to be in a tearing hurry. Maybe they were sailing sooner than they had expected.

Nat hailed him. "Any news?"

For a moment Gibaut stared at Nat as though he didn't see him. Then he spoke through his teeth. "That Elias Hasket Derby! Of all the stubborn fools that ever

. . . I wouldn't command the *Henry* if he gave her to me!"

Nat gulped. "You — you — aren't commanding the *Henry?*"

"No!" Gibaut bellowed.

"But — but — do you know who is?"

"I don't know and I don't care!" And Gibaut strode toward the ship, bellowing directions to the men to bear a hand with his gear.

Dazed, Nat left the wharf. Still in a daze, he went to his room. Now what would he do?

All that long night, until the pale winter sun rose, Nat tossed and turned and hunted for an answer. What would he do with his venture? Almost every cent he had in the world was tied up in it. And now — Gibaut was not commanding the *Henry!*

CHAPTER 12

DOWN TO THE SEA

Nat got up tireder than he had gone to bed, and still without an answer to his questions. What should he do with his venture? Try to take it back to the man who sold him the shoes? Try to send it on another ship? Ask Mr. Derby if he could send his venture on the *Henry?*

At ten that morning a message called him to Mr. Derby's office. When Nat got there he found Mr. Derby talking to a tall, sturdy man with bold, black eyes — Captain Henry Prince. Nat smiled when he saw Prince. He remembered the times the captain had been in the chandlery. When Captain Prince laughed he rattled the instruments on the shelves!

What a difference, Nat thought, between Mr. Derby and the men who commanded his ships. The Derby captains walked with a swagger and roared commands. Mr. Derby was cool and quiet. Men said Elias Derby could see around corners and guess what was coming next. A man of ideas — Mr. Derby — who knew how to pick the men to carry out his ideas.

"Nathaniel," said Mr. Derby, "Captain Prince is commanding a ship of mine — the *Henry* — on a voyage to Bourbon. He agrees with me that you'd make an excellent clerk."

Just like that! Not a word about the trouble with Gibaut! Nat tried to sound as cool and collected as Mr. Derby. "I'd like to ship as clerk under Captain Prince, sir."

"Clerk — and second mate," Prince growled. "I never carry idlers on my ship! Between ports, a clerk isn't worth the hardtack to keep him alive." He turned to Mr. Derby. "Anything else, sir?"

Mr. Derby leaned back and matched his finger tips. "Just this, Captain Prince — which I tell all my masters — every time they sail. When you're off soundings, you're on your own. I've given you suggestions for trading when you reach Bourbon. But when you get there, you may find my suggestions aren't worth the paper they're written on. You'll use your own judgment. There are only two things I expressly forbid. You'll never break a law of any port you enter. And you'll never — *never* enter into slave trade." He leaned forward, gripping the arms of his chair. "I'd rather lose any ship I own than to have it become a slaver! There is no excuse that I'd accept. Even if a slaver attacked you, overpowered you, and ordered you to carry a cargo of slaves — even that would be no excuse! You'd go down fighting — but you wouldn't turn a Derby ship into a slaver!"

Before Nat realized what he was doing, he clapped his hands. "Good for you!" Captain Prince stared at him. He felt his face get hot.

A frosty twinkle touched Mr. Derby's eyes. "I'm glad we agree, Nathaniel." He stood. "Well, gentlemen, I believe that is all."

Captain Prince and Nat left the office together. Prince clapped his hand on Nat's shoulder. "Glad you're sailing with me, Nat."

Nat explained about his venture. "It's a pretty sizable bit of cargo, sir. I invested nearly all the money I have in it — almost a hundred and thirty-five dollars."

"A hundred and . . ." Prince chuckled. "Don't worry, Nat. There's plenty of room for your venture. A hundred and thirty-five dollars . . ." Still chuckling, he waved good-by and strode off.

Nat didn't see the captain again until the raw January morning when the *Henry* was ready to sail. He was waiting on deck with the rest of the crew when he saw Captain Prince striding along the wharf. Nat grinned to himself, thinking of Prince's laughter. "He must really shake the timbers of a ship!"

Captain Prince came on board, grim-jawed, frowning. His black eyes whipped a glance over the deck, seeing everything, looking at no one. Nat gulped. Something must be wrong. Had Prince had a quarrel with Mr. Derby, too?

Captain Prince spoke to Mr. Collins, his first mate — a tall, rangy man with a lean face and cool gray eyes. Soon came the hoarse cry, "All hands! Up anchor!" All around him, men leaped to their duties, spreading sails, bracing the yards. Men walked round the capstan, leaning on the bars, heaving the anchor. Then, "Anchor's aweigh!" And the *Henry* was moving out to sea.

That evening in the middle of the dog watch, Captain Prince took his departure from Cape Ann. Navigation, Nat thought, was like surveying, all right. In surveying, you started from a known point and ran your lines by compass. In navigation, you took your departure from a known point, too, and steered your course by compass. But there the likeness ended.

Taking sights wouldn't be the same. In surveying, the earth was firm beneath your telescope. You could take all the time you wanted to check and recheck a sight. If you thought you had made a mistake, you could go back and do it over again. Here at sea, nothing would ever hold quite still. When you shot the sun at noon, you'd have one instant to get it and get it right.

And measuring your distances wouldn't be the same, either. In surveying, your chainmen could measure your distances for you. Here on the open sea, you'd measure your distance by checking your speed, and multiplying that by how long you had sailed that fast. "Many a man," Sam Smith had said, "sails halfway around the world by log, lead, and lookout." The log checked the speed, the lookout warned of dangers they could see, and the lead warned of dangers beneath the surface of the water — sudden shoals and reefs where they might go aground. He really knew a good bit about a ship, Nat thought, even though this was his first voyage.

Mr. Collins called all hands on deck to be divided into watches.

I know what the watches are, too, Nat thought. A watch is four hours: eight to midnight, midnight to four, and four to eight in the morning; then eight till noon, and noon till four. Then the next watch is the dog watch; it's divided into two watches; four to six and six to eight. Dividing the dog watch that way switches the hours of the watches for the next twenty-four, so that the same men don't stand two watches every night.

Mr. Collins was calling a man's name. The fellow nodded and moved to the larboard rail. Nat was thinking: I know about bells, too. One bell sounds the first half hour after the watch begins; two bells mark the next half hour, and so on until . . . Yes, I know a good bit about a ship. I know the —

Mr. Collins said, "Your choice, Mr. Bowditch. A man for your starboard watch."

Nat gulped and his brains began to spin. He had known he would stand watch, but he hadn't realized he'd command a watch. With his thoughts still in a whirl he said, "Chad Jensen."

Old Chad said, "Aye, aye sir!" and moved to the starboard side. Mr. Collins chose again. It was Nat's turn once more. "Dan Keeler."

He felt Mr. Collins' surprise. He was surprised at himself. Why had he chosen Dan Keeler? Dan was a troublemaker who'd been spread-eagled for twelve lashes many times.

Dan Keeler slewed a sidelong stare at Nat. "Aye, aye, sir," he rumbled. His glance seemed to say, You lubberly little runt!

When the crew had been divided into watches, Captain Prince came topside and stood on the quarter-deck, staring down at the men. He was still in a temper, Nat thought. Funny, what anger could do to a man. He looked ten years older than he had that day in Derby's office.

The captain began to speak. His words bit like the lash of a whip. It did not take him long to tell the men what he expected of them, and what would happen if they did not obey on the double. He finished, wheeled, and strode below.

They heaved the log and set the course. Eight bells. Mr. Collins said, "Lay below the larboard watch!"

And Nat stood on the deck of the *Henry,* in command of the first watch. With a hollow feeling where his stomach should have been he stared miserably about him. Old Chad Jensen was taking the first trick at the wheel. Thank goodness he knew someone. He went over and stood at Chad's shoulder, watching the compass in the glow on the binnacle light. Good old Chad. He'd known him ever since his first days at the chandlery, when he used to drop in between voyages and spin yarns with Sam Smith.

Nat said, "You steer a straight course, Chad."

Chad's eyes did not move. His gaze was fixed on the compass. "Aye, aye, sir. Thank you, Mr. Bowditch."

The hollow feeling hit Nat's stomach again. Was he going to spend months — maybe a year — with men who acted as though they had never seen him before? He paced the deck and then stared miserably over the rail.

"Mr. Bowditch." Captain Prince was standing by him.

"Aye, aye, sir!"

"In any emergency, call me. Remember, a captain

always sleeps with one ear cocked." He wheeled and
went below again.

His voice was still grim. He seemed to be speaking
from the other side of a gulf that Nat could never cross.
But Nat felt comforted.

At eight bells, when Mr. Collins relieved him, Nat
stumbled below, surprised to find he was utterly ex-
hausted. What had he done? Nothing. Just stayed on
the alert, watching for emergencies. He threw himself
into his bunk with his clothes on. "I know what that is,
too," he muttered, "when you tumble in with your
clothes on. You turn in *all standing*. Yes, I know a lot,
I do!"

It seemed to him he had scarcely dozed off when confusion topside wakened him. He heard feet thudding
across the deck, and men shouting. Someone banged on
a hatch and bellowed, "All hands on deck!"

Nat stumbled topside. As he emerged from the hatchway, the wind almost took him off his feet. The *Henry*
was rolling heavily, shipping water with every roll.

The rest of that night, and for six days and nights that
followed, Nat found out what men meant by the Roaring
Forties of the North Atlantic. Numb with weariness, he
lived in wet clothes and ate cold food. It was bad enough
on deck; it was worse below deck. The hatchways had to
be closed, and below deck the air grew so foul that the
very lanterns burned dim. Whenever Nat had to go below, the stench grabbed at his throat and turned his
stomach. Why, he wondered, had he ever wanted to
come to sea? Why did any man choose this life?

It was all right maybe for a man who became a captain — but what about men like Keeler and Jensen — who'd spent their lives in the fo'c'sle? Why would they live like this for salt beef, hardtack, and twelve dollars a month?

The sixth night, just before midnight, Nat went on deck for his watch. The storm had ended; the sky glittered with stars. Nat caught his breath and stared. No man, he thought, had ever seen stars until he had seen them from a ship in mid-ocean.

The next morning, just after seven bells of the forenoon watch, Captain Prince came on deck with his sextant, ready to shoot the sun. "Have you ever used a sextant, Mr. Bowditch?"

"Not at sea, sir. But I have one."

"Then get it."

"Aye, aye, sir!" Nat hurried below for his sextant and slate. If he could just do this smartly and well, maybe Prince wouldn't be so grim. He hurried topside, fumbled his sextant out of its case, and dropped the case. He flushed, and didn't pick it up. He leveled the sextant to catch the horizon, and started to bring the sun into focus.

Captain Prince drawled, "Don't you think you'll need a shade, Mr. Bowditch?"

Nat felt his ears burn. He fumbled the red glass into place. When the sun reached its zenith and stood still the fractional moment, Nat took his reading. He checked in the almanac. His slate pencil streaked through his figuring. Captain Prince stood watching him.

When Nat had finished, he said, "Hmmm. You are quick at figures, Mr. Bowditch. Well, we've got our latitude, all right. The longitude — that's something else again. I wish chronometers weren't so infernally expensive."

Nat said, "How about a lunar, sir? Won't that give you your longitude?"

Prince shrugged. "Once in a blue moon you can get one, but by the time you've worked out all your computations, it's about two days later. You may find out where you were, but you'll never know where you are."

"I don't think the mathematics would take quite that long, sir," Nat said. "I'd like to try taking a lunar, first chance we have."

Prince shrugged again. "Go ahead. Be handy to know our longitude. If we could be sure." He didn't sound as though he thought much of the idea.

Nat checked his nautical almanac closely, hunting for the first night the moon promised to be in a good position for a lunar. That night he went on deck before the time for his watch, with his sextant.

Little Johnny, the cabin boy, joined him. "Mr. Bowditch, sir, would you tell me what you're going to do?"

"Of course, Johnny. I'm trying to find out a little more about where we are. We know our latitude — how far north of the equator we are. The trick is to find our longitude — how far east or west we are."

"East or west of where?" Johnny asked; then, hastily, "Sir?"

"That's a good question, Johnny. First, we have to pick a north-south line to be east or west of. And since we used to belong to England, we use the same line that the English use — the north-south line through London. We call it the meridian of London."

"But how can we ever figure how far west of London

we are — when we're here — and London is away off somewhere else?"

"We have to figure that by time," Nat told him.

Johnny stared. "Time? Mr. Bowditch, sir, is that a joke?"

"No, Johnny. Every twenty-four hours, the earth turns around once. So the sun seems to be rising somewhere, every hour — even every minute. When it's sunrise in London, we know it's sunset halfway around the world. And, a fourth of the way around the world, it's midnight. If we had one of those fine ship's clocks called chronometers, we could use it to tell how far from London we are. We'd keep it set to London time. In the morning, when we checked our sunrise, we'd look at the clock and see what time it was in London, and we could figure how far from London we were, because we know how many miles the earth turns every hour."

"But we don't have one of those — uh — uh — special clocks, do we?"

"No, Johnny. So I'm going to check our position by the moon. You see, we know by the nautical almanac exactly where the moon will be — every hour, every minute, every second. And we know where a great many of the brightest stars will be. So, if we can catch the moon as it crosses in front of a certain star — we call it 'occulting' the star — we can figure how far away from London we are when we see it happen."

"That sounds easier," Johnny declared.

Nat grinned. "Most people don't think so. There's quite a little figuring to do. But the big problem is to catch the moon crossing in front of a star that is bright enough for us to still see the star when it's that close to the moon. There ought to be some better way to work a lunar — but we don't have it — yet."

Johnny stared at Nat's sextant and sighed. "I wish some time I could look through a sextant."

"You can," Nat said. "The moon's going to be bright enough tonight for us to catch the horizon. I'll teach you to check Polaris — the North Star."

The next night, when Nat came topside before his watch, Keeler approached him. "Mr. Bowditch, sir, is it true that you let Johnny look through your sextant? Or was the little lubber lying to us?"

"He did try his hand with the sextant. Would you like to?"

"Me?" Keeler gulped. "You mean — *me?*"

"Why not?"

"But — but — nothing, sir."

That night Keeler had his turn at hearing about the moon and trying to check the angle of Polaris.

Then one evening during the dog watch, before the stars were visible, Nat leveled his sextant to catch the horizon. Johnny was at his elbow.

"Mr. Bowditch, sir, what are you doing now?"

"I'm sighting a star."

Johnny turned a puzzled glance to Nat. "But there aren't any stars."

"Yes, there are, Johnny. There are always stars. We just can't see them until it's dark enough for them to show. When you want to get an angle on a star, and we don't have bright moonlight, the problem is to get the horizon when it's light enough to see it, and to get the star when it's dark enough to see it. So I'm starting to check the star while I can still see the horizon. And I'm watching where I know the star will be when I can see it."

The men gathered round to listen. From that night on, the dog watch was Nat's busy time. Even Herbie, the huge Negro cook, wanted to hear Mr. Bowditch talk about the stars.

"Daggone," Herbie said, "it kind of picks a fellow up to think about the stars. Kind of makes you forget about soaking the salt beef till it's fitten to eat, and about smelling the bilge water." He shook his head and grinned. "Just think of me learning things! Me!"

"Of course you can learn," Nat told him. "Every one of you can learn."

But teaching them wasn't so easy. Time and again Nat explained something in the simplest words he could think of — only to see a blank look on the man's face. Time and again he wanted to shout, "Can't you see? Can't you understand anything?" But he always remembered Elizabeth Boardman and the parallel rulers. He always remembered how she said, "Your brain — it's too fast. So you stumble on other people's dumbness — like a chair in the dark. And you want to kick something."

He would bite back his impatience. Slowly, carefully, he'd explain again — and again. At last he'd see the man's eyes brighten. He'd hear the happy, "Oh, yes! Simple, isn't it?" Nat would grin. "Yes — simple."

When he got back to his cabin, he would write down the explanation that had finally made sense to a man. Just so I won't forget it, if I ever have to explain that again! he told himself. After three weeks, he had quite a stack of notes. He was making a new notebook, he realized; a very different sort of notebook. All his other notebooks just said enough to explain things to him. But this notebook said everything he had to say to explain things to other men — to the men who sailed before the mast.

Weeks passed. Nat saw much more of the fo'c'sle and the cabin boy than he did of the captain, first mate, and their passenger. Captain Prince, Mr. Collins, and Monsieur Bonnefoy dined together. The second mate dined alone, after they had eaten. Nat didn't mind. At first he read at the table. But after he started teaching the men, he spent all his time at mess answering Johnny's questions. It helped — to explain things to Johnny. After he'd made Johnny understand, Nat didn't have to go over things so many times to make the men in the fo'c'sle understand.

One day Captain Prince called Nat to his cabin. The captain's grimness had not relaxed. "Tell me, Mr. Bowditch, just what are you trying to do with the men during the dog watch?"

"Teach them what they want to know, sir."

Captain Prince cocked an eyebrow. "And can learn?"

"They finally get it, sir," Nat told him, "if I just find the right way to explain it."

"But, Mr. Bowditch, why are you doing it?"

Nat was silent for a moment. "Maybe, sir, it's because I want to pay a debt I owe to the men who helped me; men like Sam Smith and Dr. Bentley and Dr. Prince and Nathan Read. Maybe that's why. Or maybe it's just because of the men. We have good men before the mast, Captain Prince. Every man of them could be a first mate — if he knew navigation."

Captain Prince muttered something under his breath. "An odd business!" he said. "But I've never had less trouble with a crew. Carry on, Mr. Bowditch."

"Aye, aye, sir."

Someone tapped on the door, and Monsieur Bonnefoy entered, smiling. "I have a confession to make, Captain Prince. I was eavesdropping through the skylight. Not by intention. I just happened to be there, and could not help hearing. Monsieur Bowditch — he has the magnificent spirit! It is worthy of the French Revolution! Liberty! Equality! Fraternity!"

Captain Prince roared, "What do you mean — the French Revolution? Who started this business of rebelling against kings? We did! We started it in 1775! It took you French until 1789 to get around to it!" Then, for the first time since the *Henry* had sailed, Nat saw a twinkle in Prince's eyes.

Monsieur Bonnefoy apologized. He was so embarrassed and he talked so fast that he started talking French. Without thinking, Nat answered him in French.

Bonnefoy beamed. "Monsieur! You speak French! Why didn't you tell me?"

"I — I — guess I just didn't think of it."

Captain Prince roared again. "So you didn't think of it? And here I've been expecting all along I'd have to have an interpreter in Bourbon! Have you any more tricks up your sleeve, Mr. Bowditch?"

"No, sir, I — I — don't think so, sir."

"No more languages?"

"Just — just — Latin, sir. I learned that to read Newton's *Principia*."

Prince mimicked him. *"Just Latin; to read* Principia. And you still think it's worth your time to teach those poor devils in the fo'c'sle?"

"Yes, sir, I do!" Nat snapped.

Captain Prince gave him a long, hard stare. "Carry on, Mr. Bowditch. That's all."

Almost three months out of Salem, the *Henry* reached the Cape of Good Hope, and ran into more bad weather. For three days and nights they fought head winds, trying to make their easting. Again the men lived in wet clothes and ate cold food, and turned to all standing, because they knew they'd be called out again soon by the bellow, "All hands on deck!"

"I wonder who named this the Cape of Good Hope?" Nat said.

Prince growled, "The Portygee explorers named it right — Cape *Tempestuoso* — the Cape of Storms. But I guess their king didn't like the sound of that. After all, he was interested in trade with the east. So he changed it to Cape of Good Hope."

Nat said, "I suppose Hope fits — in a way. You can always *hope* you'll get around it."

"Double it, Mr. Bowditch!" Prince roared. "You don't *get around* a cape! You *double it!* You — you — lubber!"

"Aye, aye, sir." Nat smiled to himself. He knew just how Prince felt. It was a relief to know he wasn't the only man who ever stumbled on someone's dumbness — like a chair in the dark — and wanted to kick something.

One night early in May Nat got a good lunar observation and worked out their longitude. He went to Prince's cabin. "According to my figures, sir, we're sixty-one miles east of our dead reckoning."

Captain Prince shook his head. "We couldn't have overrun our reckoning that much!"

"If my figures are right, sir, at our present speed, we'll sight Bourbon on the eighth."

Prince drawled, "So, Mr. Bowditch? I wouldn't put on my go-ashore clothes if I were you."

It was during Nat's watch early the morning of the eighth when he heard the lookout's singsong, "Land, ho-o-o-o-o-o!"

Captain Prince came on deck. He said, "Hmmmm . . ." He rubbed his chin and swept Nat with a sidelong glance. "I believe you can work a lunar, Mr. Bowditch."

"Of course," Nat said. "It's a simple matter of mathematics, sir."

Captain Prince said, "Hmmmm" again and returned to his cabin.

Nat stared across the water until the rugged peaks of Bourbon loomed on the horizon. Bourbon — where they'd sell their cargo for double its cost — or lose their shirts. For the first time in months, Nat thought of his venture. What would happen to his cargo of shoes in Bourbon? Would he win — or lose? He watched the ragged outline take shape in the mist. Bourbon . . .

CHAPTER 13

DISCOVERY

Monsieur Bonnefoy hurried on deck and stood at the rail. "Ah, Bourbon!" he sighed. Then he snapped his fingers impatiently. "No, no! I must remember! Since the Revolution, all is changed! It is no longer Bourbon — cursed name of kings! It is Réunion. And I must remember to call every man Citizen! We no no longer have titles. No *Monsieur!* No *Marquis!* Every man is Citizen!"

When they were still well out from shore, a pilot boat came to meet the *Henry,* and the pilot conducted them to anchorage a mile off Bourbon. Nat spoke to the man in French. When would they be allowed to enter the harbor?

The pilot shrugged and spread his hands. "There is no harbor, monsieur. The last typhoon — *pouff!* It took everything!"

Nat interpreted to Captain Prince.

Prince said, "The devil! That means we'll have to lighter the cargo."

The pilot explained the situation cheerfully. Nat translated again. "He says it will really not delay us much — having to lighter the cargo. The coffee crop is slow coming in. Even if we unloaded quickly, we'd have to wait on our return cargo. So everything is working out fine — he says."

Captain Prince said, "He still calls it Bourbon, doesn't he?"

"Yes. I asked him about that. He says the people are used to saying Bourbon. They haven't gotten around to changing yet."

Another American ship was anchored near the *Henry*. The master, Captain Blanchard, came aboard the *Henry*. He was full of questions about home and just as full of advice about how to get along in Bourbon.

"Remember the Revolution!" he said. "Call every man Citizen! Say *Vive la république!* That's what I did! And do you know what happened? Those Frenchies were so pleased that they bought my whole cargo of wine — just like that! At one thousand livres a cask!"

Prince thanked Blanchard for his advice.

"It's nothing," Blanchard said. "Glad to help you. Remember! *Vive la république!* And you'll sell your cargo in jig time!"

The next day Captain Prince, Nat, and Monsieur Bonnefoy went ashore. When they landed, Bonnefoy spoke to everyone he saw, calling loudly and cheerfully, *"Bon jour, Citoyen!"*

The people smiled, answered lazily, *"Bon jour, monsieur!"*

It didn't seem to Nat that they were worrying much about the Revolution. In fact, they didn't seem to be worrying much about anything. How slowly they moved, walking as though they had just gotten over a long illness!

Before Nat had gone far, though, he found out why people moved so lazily. They had the right idea. Brisk dashing about didn't work well in the muggy tropical heat.

They told Monsieur Bonnefoy good-by, and went to the Office of the Committee of Public Safety to get permission to land their cargo. Near the office, a man greeted them and offered his services as an interpreter. Nat was glad now that Frederic Jordy had made him learn to pronounce French. For Prince clapped his hand on Nat's shoulder and said, "We don't need an interpreter!"

Nat handled their business quickly, while Captain Prince relaxed and waited.

When business was settled, one of the Frenchmen said, "Did you hear about Captain Blanchard, monsieur?" His eyes twinkled. "He tried to impress us. He shouted, *'Vive la république!'* So — of course we were impressed. It would have been rude not to be, eh? We offered him one thousand livres per cask for his whole cargo of wine. We bought it all, too. He didn't know . . ." For a moment the Frenchman laughed so hard he could not go on. "He didn't know that wine is so scarce it's selling for *five* thousand livres a cask!"

Nat laughed with him, then pulled a solemn face. "Citizen! I have some shoes to sell! *Vive la république!*"

The Frenchmen laughed and slapped each other on the shoulders. "You'll easily get three hundred fifty livres for boots," they told him, "if you don't try to impress anyone!"

Nat did some rapid calculating. A livre was worth about three cents now. If he did as well on the half boots and shoes, too, he'd sell his venture for four times what he paid for it!

The next day the long, tedious business of lightering their cargo began. Some days they unloaded seventy-five casks; some days the sea was so rough that they had to cover the water with an oil slick before the boats could approach the *Henry*. Some days the rain came in torrents and they could do nothing. A whole month to lighter a cargo that could have been unloaded in days at a wharf!

Every day Johnny's face got longer. "I hope," he muttered, "it isn't going to take this long to load!"

But it did. There were days when the sun was bright and the sea was calm — and there was no coffee ready to be loaded. There were other days when a cargo waited on shore — and the rain poured down. It was September — with luck they'd have been home then — before they weighed anchor.

Nat watched the jagged outlines of Bourbon fade astern. He saw Prince's face harden into grim lines again. Why was it, he wondered. He puzzled over it, but couldn't find an answer.

Soon his days and nights settled down to a routine. As second mate, he stood watches; he was doing most of the navigating now. Everyone admitted he could shoot the sun as well as the next man, and do the figuring afterwards twice as fast. As for lunars — no one else pretended to work those calculations. Betweentimes, Nat taught the crew, and studied the tables in Moore's book of navigation.

One night when he was working with Moore he blinked, shook his head, and stared at a figure again. That couldn't be a mistake in Moore! Moore's *Navigator* was supposed to be the best book of its kind in the world! Nat worked through the figures twice to be sure; it was an error! He was so startled that he strode into Captain Prince's cabin without knocking.

Captain Prince jumped to his feet. "What's happened?

"I found an error in one of Moore's tables!"

Prince looked at him in utter disgust. "Is that what you came slamming in here about? An error in which table?"

Nat told him.

Prince gave a short laugh. "My dear Mr. Bowditch, Moore didn't compute that table. Do you know who did? Nevil Maskelyne, the royal astronomer of England!"

"I can't help who computed it!" Nat barked. "There's an error!" He showed Prince his page of figures. "There! I checked it! See? Why didn't Moore check those figures before he accepted them?"

Prince looked at the paper covered with Nat's tiny figures. "All that — to find one error? And there are probably two hundred thousand figures in those tables. Maybe that's why he didn't check every figure, Mr. Bowditch."

"But he should have! Mathematics is nothing if it isn't accurate! Men's lives depend on the accuracy of those tables! It's — it's — criminal to have a mistake in a book like this! Do you hear me! It's criminal! Men's lives depend on these figures!" Nat hadn't realized how he was shouting until he stopped. In the heavy silence he heard the *bong-bong* of the ship's bell.

Captain Prince said, "Eight bells. Your watch, Mr. Bowditch. Men's lives depend on that, too."

"Aye, aye, sir." Nat went topside. Furiously he paced the deck. Then, as suddenly as his temper blazed, he cooled off and laughed at himself. What a fool he had been to storm at Captain Prince that way. It wasn't Prince's fault there were errors in Moore's book! When he saw Prince again, he'd apologize.

All through his watch he caught himself listening for Prince's footstep or his voice. But he did not appear. When Nat's watch ended, he went below with a lantern to get his sextant. He found a note lying on the copy of Moore's book. In Prince's slashing scrawl he read:

Carry on, Mr. Bowditch! Find some more errors, and we'll beard Mr. Blunt of Newbury in his den when we get home. He's the American publisher who's going to bring out an American edition of Moore.

Nat grinned and went topside again with his sextant. Tonight ought to be a good one for a lunar. The moon was due to pass over a star that was bright enough to see in spite of its nearness to the moon. But the same thing happened that happened so many times. Just when the moon neared the bright star, a cloud got in the way. Nat shrugged and sighed. There ought to be a better way to work a lunar! He studied the glittering heavens. Was there another star bright enough tonight — that the moon would pass over? Of course not. He knew that.

That one . . . the moon would pass below it . . . that one
. . . the moon would pass above it . . . that one . . .

The idea hit Nat so suddenly that he gasped. He raced
below and for the second time that night crashed into
Prince's cabin without knocking.

Prince was asleep, but he was on his feet in an instant.
"What is it?"

"A new way to work lunars! Come on deck! As fast as
you can!" He dashed out the door and up the companionway. He was on deck again before he remembered he hadn't said *sir*. When Prince joined him, Nat's
words tumbled over themselves as he explained. "This
business of waiting for the moon to occult a star — it's a
nuisance. But what if we take the position of the moon
in relation to three stars? For instance, right now, we
can get the angle between — "

Captain Prince said, "Wait!" He sent for his sextant.
"Mr. Collins, swing into the wind, back sail and hold
steady!"

Soon they were checking lunars the new way. When
they had taken several sights, they went below. Nat
checked the stars in the almanac and made his computations. His method worked!

Nat glowed. "See? That's mathematics! It should
give you the right answer!"

Prince sighed. "Yes, Mr. Bowditch. And now —
please — no more discoveries tonight!"

"Aye, aye, sir!" Nat laughed and went topside again.
He was too excited to sleep.

When the *Henry* anchored in Salem Harbor, Nat went
with Captain Prince to the Custom House to declare
their cargo.

As they came out, Prince laughed and clapped Nat on the back. "A good voyage, Nat!" He grinned like a boy again. "The *Henry* did well — and so did you!"

"Aye, aye, sir! Mighty well!" He had his pay, and almost five hundred dollars that he had made on his venture in shoes. And he had his new way of working lunars. Ho for the life of a sailor! he thought. He caught himself walking with a bit of a roll.

The cold of the North Atlantic, the smothering heat of the tropics, the days and nights of fighting storms — all seemed very far away now.

He saw a pudgy figure hurrying to meet them. "There's Dr. Bentley!" He lifted his hand to wave and call, but something in the minister's face silenced him.

Dr. Bentley said, "Nat, you must see Mary first. She needs you. David — and his crew — all died of fever."

CHAPTER 14

NINETEEN GUNS

David — and his crew — all died of fever!
Heartsick, Nat hurried to Mary's house. All the way
there his thoughts were a jumble. What could he say to
Mary? How could he comfort her?

"Maybe if I waited till after supper," he muttered, "I
could think of something to say." But he knew he was
being a coward to tell himself that. He reached the
house, tapped, and opened the door.

Lois was there with Mary, helping Mary's little daughter read her *New England Primer*.

Mary saw Nat first. "Nat!" She came to meet him.
"Dear Nat!" Her lips trembled and her eyes filled with
tears. For a moment she leaned her forehead against his
shoulder, hiding her face. "If it hadn't been for you,
Nat, I wouldn't have married David."

"I know," Nat admitted miserably. He'd been thinking of that, himself.

"Did Dr. Bentley tell you I wanted to see you?"

"Yes, Mary. I came right away."

"I wanted to say *thank you,* Nat. If it hadn't been for
you, I would have missed being the happiest woman in
Salem — while David was here." She lifted her head.
Her lips were steady now; she smiled slightly. "Thank
you, Nat. And now . . . will you do something for me?"

"Anything I can."

"Sit down here, and tell us all about your voyage —
everything — just as David used to when he came home."

Three hours later, supper was over, the dishes washed,
and Nat was still talking. Someone called, the door
opened, and Elizabeth Boardman came in with her cousin,
Mary Ingersoll, whom all the family called Polly.

Elizabeth's violet eyes glowed. "I heard you were
here!"

Polly's level brown eyes danced with mischief. "I think
Elizabeth was just going to drop in to see Mary — and
pretend to be surprised when she saw you — but she was
afraid I'd tell on her!"

Elizabeth blushed and laughed. "Children!" she said.

Polly made a face. "You're not so old! Sixteen! And
I'm almost!"

Elizabeth laughed with Polly. She said, "Tell us all
about everything, Nat!"

Nat was solemn. "I couldn't possibly. It's taken me
three hours to tell Mary and Lois — and I haven't got
them off Bourbon yet. Little girls shouldn't stay up that
late."

This time Polly made a face at him. "When Father comes home, I stay up till all hours!" Nat could imagine that. Polly's father was Captain Ingersoll, one of the most famous captains who sailed a Derby ship.

He told them about Bourbon, and Captain Blanchard's *Vive la république.* At nine, he walked to the Boardman house with them, and then went to see Dr. Bentley.

Dr. Bentley talked late, bringing Nat up to date on the news of nations. Nat listened hungrily. He remembered how Hab had once said, "When I get home from a voyage, I feel as though I had been asleep six months."

Affairs were in a miserable tangle, Dr. Bentley said. Things weren't settled with England yet. Americans were still fighting the Jay Treaty bitterly. English captains were still searching our vessels and seizing our sailors. And the trouble with France grew more serious every day. "I doubt if you'll be sailing soon again, Nat. At least not until the trouble with France is settled."

But a few days later Mr. Derby called Nat and Captain Prince to his office to talk over another voyage. "The ship is named the *Astrea.*" He smiled slightly. "I rather like that name."

Nat thought of the earlier *Astrea,* on which Captain John Derby had brought the news of peace from Paris. He remembered how proud he'd been when his father said, "Crowded sail, he did, and came from Paris in twenty-two days!"

Mr. Derby seemed to be reading Nat's thoughts. "The other *Astrea* made a record for herself. I intend that this *Astrea* shall set a record, too; the first Salem ship ever to enter Manila Harbor!"

Manila! Halfway around the world! Evidently, Nat decided, Mr. Derby wasn't too concerned about the trouble with France.

Mr. Derby went on in his quiet way. "The *Astrea* mounts nineteen guns, Captain Prince. If any of your crew has ever shipped on a privateer or a letter of marque ship they — ah — might be useful."

Nat's scalp prickled.

Captain Prince merely nodded. "Any ports before Manila?"

"Yes. You'll carry a mixed cargo to Lisbon, and stop at Funchal, in the Madeira Islands. Then on to Manila."

When Nat and Captain Prince left the office, Nat said, "Manila . . . I wonder what language they talk there?"

"The Spanish are the . . . " Prince stared at Nat. "Don't tell me you're going to learn another language?"

"Why not . . . sir?"

Prince pursed his lips and shook his head. "Carry on, Mr. Bowditch."

A few days later Nat was ready to start learning Spanish; he had a dictionary, a grammar, and a New Testament. He opened the New Testament to the first chapter of John. Again he repeated the words in English: In the beginning was the Word, and the Word was with God and the Word was God. He looked at the Spanish: *En el principio era el Verbo, y el Verbo era con Dios, y el Verbo era Dios.* Nat smiled. Spanish, he decided, would be the easiest language of all to learn. He could figure out every word in the sentence without a bit of trouble.

Toward the last of March Mary said, "Do you have to sail Friday, Nat?"

Nat teased her. "You're not superstitious about Friday, are you?"

"Saturday's your birthday. If you do have to sail Friday, I wish — "

Nat saw the idea back of Mary's eyes. "Oh, no! You don't tell anyone that Saturday is my birthday!"

"Why not?"

"I wouldn't care for a celebration on shipboard."

"Why? What would they do?"

"Oh — something jolly — like ducking me or pouring a few buckets of water on me. No celebrations, please!"

Mary promised she'd keep his birthday a dark secret. Nat kissed her and went down to the wharf to see how the loading of the *Astrea* was coming along.

Mr. Collins was on board, and in a foul humor. "You and your teaching!" he growled.

"What's wrong with my teaching?"

"We've lost four of the men we were counting on — including Keeler!"

Nat grinned. "Keeler was supposed to be a trouble-maker, wasn't he? I'd think you'd be relieved."

"He was," Collins growled, "but Keeler knew guns. Blast you and your teaching! Four good men all signed up as second mates on smaller vessels!"

"Good for them!"

Collins glared. "What about us?"

"We'll just have to replace them."

"Sure. Just like that. And do you know who is going to replace Keeler? Lem Harvey!"

Nat whistled. He knew Lem Harvey — a huge fellow

with hulking shoulders and a sullen, swarthy face. A troublemaker if ever one lived. "Why sign him on?"

"Because," Collins growled, "he sailed on privateers before he was knee high to a capstan. He knows guns. If we have trouble with the French he'll be worth the rest of the crew put together."

"And if we don't have trouble with the French?" Nat asked.

"We'll have trouble with Lem. Personally, I'd rather have trouble with the French!"

A boy came aboard with a letter for Nat.

Dear Nat
    Good luck on your voyage. When the *Astrea* sails, I'm going to be on the captain's walk, watching you.
                                              ELIZABETH

Early Friday morning Nat strolled across the Common toward the big white house and saw Elizabeth standing on the captain's walk. She waved and signaled that she'd come down. A few moments later she came outside to meet him.

"You're shivering," Nat said. "You're cold."

"I'm not cold," she whispered, "I'm scared!" Her violet eyes looked bigger than ever in her heart-shaped face. "Nat, they have *guns* on the *Astrea!* Why?"

"Just so we won't have any trouble. If a French privateer sees us, we'll look so dangerous the privateer will crowd sail and run!"

Elizabeth didn't smile. "Nat, please take care of yourself. If you — if anything — " Suddenly she stood on tiptoe, kissed him, wheeled, and fled into the house.

Nat stared after her. He started to follow. He stopped. Nonsense, he told himself. She's just a child. Get on board your ship, Mr. Bowditch! He strode briskly toward the waterfront.

Somehow — he didn't quite know how it happened — he found himself on Union Wharf instead of Derby, and had to pretend he was looking for someone.

Once the *Astrea* had weighed anchor, though, he forgot about everything behind him. He even forgot about sixteen-year-olds who did unexpected things — such as kissing a man good-by. For the wind was against them. If the *Astrea* managed to beat out of Salem Harbor, every man on board was going to need four arms and six pairs of hands to handle sail.

The men worked desperately to keep her far enough into the wind to clear Naugus Head. But they couldn't make it. They had to come to and anchor again. All day Friday and Friday night, they stood their watches and slept with their ears cocked; all day Saturday and all that night and all Sunday morning they waited. It was late Sunday afternoon before they finally got under way.

Again they divided the men into watches.

When Nat had his first choice, he heard himself say, "Lem Harvey!" And then wondered why he did it. Was it because he felt responsible for Lem's being on the *Astrea?*

When the watches were divided, Captain Prince stood on the quarter-deck and spoke to the crew. If anything, he sounded grimmer than he had sounded on the *Henry.* He added something to what he had said then: "There are two things every man of you must learn and learn fast. First, you'll learn to recognize the colors of every nation. When you're on lookout and you sight a sail, you'll take it for granted it's an enemy until you know it's a friend. Second, you must learn to handle these guns like the crew of a man-o'-war. Lem Harvey, I'm putting you in charge of training the crew on the guns. I want these men drilled until they can cast loose their guns, run them out, and fire — " he snapped his fingers — "like that! Do you understand?"

Lem Harvey didn't smile, or straighten, or show any pleasure. He scowled, his heavy black brows coming together over his sullen eyes. "Aye, aye, sir. They'll learn . . . " That was all he said aloud. But Nat saw his mouth finish the sentence. "They'll learn, or they'll wish they had!"

Day after day Nat heard Lem roar his orders and bellow his abuse. Between spates of profanity, the directions were exact:

"CAST LOOSE YOUR GUNS! No! You thumb-fingered fool! Make that muzzle lashing fast to the eye-bolt!

"LEVEL YOUR GUNS! How many times do I have to tell you — lash that bed to the bolts!

"TAKE OUT YOUR TOMPIONS! You blasted fool! Don't stand there and hold it! Drop it! What you think that lanyard's for?

"RUN OUT YOUR GUNS! You! Look at those tackle falls! What sort of lubber's coil is that? In fakes, I told you! In fakes!

"PRIME! Get that powder horn out of the way! Serve you right if I'd let you stand there till it blew up in your face! Move!

"POINT YOUR GUNS! No! First with your side

sights, and then with your upper sights! You there, ready with that match!

"FIRE!"

And the guns roared. Before the sound died and the smoke lifted, Lem was bellowing again.

"SPONGE YOUR GUNS! Where the . . . is that sponge! Ram it down! Ram it home! Twist it! You want to leave a spark in there to blow you to . . . Ready with that cartridge! What are you doing? Sleeping on your feet?

"LOAD! Get that wad in there, you fool! Ram it home! Ram it!

"SHOT YOUR GUNS!"

Day after day Lem bullied and jeered and cursed the men. But they learned to handle the guns. They finally moved fast enough to please even Captain Prince. But Lem still bullied them. When the men weren't drilling on the guns, they were slaving in the rigging.

Nat was glad for the crew when they sighted the coast of Portugal. They stood off and on all night. In the morning, a pilot came on board to take them up the Tagus River. They sailed through the mile-wide mouth of the river, and then saw the Tagus spread into a great bay. On the north bank of the river the city of Lisbon rose on the hills.

Nat stared at the houses; he'd never seen anything like them — tile roofed, and painted every color of the rainbow.

Mr. Collins drawled, "Well, Mr. Bowditch, did you learn Portygee talk, too? So you could be handy in port?"

Nat said, "Blast! I didn't think of that. I've been learning Spanish — for Manila."

But when Nat and Captain Prince went on shore, they found the custom officials conducted all their business in French. Again Captain Prince clapped his hand on Nat's shoulder and said, "We don't need an interpreter!" Soon Nat was busy changing *escudos* to dollars, and adding figures in his head before the other men could add them on paper. Betweentimes he went sightseeing in Lisbon.

I must remember all this, he thought, to tell Elizabeth when I . . . He felt his cheeks get hot. To tell all of them, I mean.

But it was Elizabeth's face, and her sparkling eyes, he could see when he thought of home. He drew rough sketches of things he wanted to remember — the tawny oxen that looked so fierce — with their six-foot spread of horns; the amazing women of Portugal, who carried everything on their heads — boxes, baskets, and huge flat trays of fish. He tried to sketch the streets of Lisbon, but he couldn't get the effect he wanted on flat paper.

I'll tell her — them — he thought, that no matter where I wanted to go, it was always uphill from where I'd been. He could imagine how Elizabeth's eyes would sparkle. "When we get back," he said . . . and he stopped.

Before they got back, the *Astrea* would have sailed halfway around the world. Lisbon might seem far from Salem now, but it was next door to home, compared to far-off Manila.

He found an old sailor who had doubled the Cape, and been to India and through Sunda Strait to Manila. With the help of a map, gestures, Spanish, and figures, Nat managed to learn a lot.

Things went quickly in Lisbon — but not quickly

enough to keep Lem from slipping ashore when he was on duty, getting into a fight, and landing in jail. He was put in the brig until the *Astrea* was ready to sail. The morning they were to weigh anchor he was released.

A storm howled in from the Atlantic, and for a week they waited out miserable days and nights. Lem tried to slip ashore again, and sat out the rest of the storm in the brig.

After a week, they managed to beat out of the Tagus, into the Atlantic. Then they battled head winds to Madeira. Lem was released from the brig again; they needed his weight on the halyards.

At last they anchored in Funchal Bay. The storm had ended; a moon rose, and they saw the whitewashed houses rising on steep hills, gleaming in the moonlight.

When Captain Prince and Nat went ashore, the first man to greet them was Mr. Pintard, the American consul. He hailed them like long-lost brothers, asked news of home, and invited them to dinner, all in one breath.

Mrs. Pintard was all smiles, too, when they dined in the Pintard home. She was full of stories of the islands. "Mr. Bowditch," she said, "have you heard that delightful legend of how Machico got its name? There were two lovers — "

Mr. Pintard smiled. "My dear, Mr. Bowditch is a mathematician, not a — Well, he'd hardly be interested in your legends."

"A mathematician? Then here's an interesting problem for you, Mr. Bowditch. Five years ago, I inherited some money in Ireland." She named the amount.

Mr. Pintard said, "Dear, wait until after dinner, and we'll let Mr. Bowditch write down — "

Nat said, "And what happened?"

"The money was invested in Ireland at eight per cent," she told him. "After three years the whole sum — interest and all — was sent to England. It was invested there at eight and a half per cent. After two years — let me see — yes, two years and two months — the whole sum was sent to me here. How much should I have received?"

Mr. Pintard said, "After dinner, dear, you can write down the whole thing for him, and he can take it home and work it out. We don't want him to waste his evening over figures, do we?"

Nat laid down his knife and fork and sat staring at the flickering lights of the candles. After a little he said, "Eight hundred and forty-three pounds, fifteen shillings, and six and one-fourth pence. Tell me about Machico."

Mrs. Pintard stared.

Mr. Pintard said, "What!"

"Machico," Nat repeated. "I'd like to hear how it got its name."

Captain Prince grinned. "Two minutes by my watch. He won't have to waste the evening after all."

"But that's right!" Mrs. Pintard gasped. "To the last fraction! That's exactly how much I received!"

"Of course," Nat told her. "That's the beauty of mathematics. It's exact. Now, about Machico . . . "

Mrs. Pintard was still staring at him, dumfounded.

"You've no idea how handy he is in port." Captain Prince was amused.

Mr. Pintard shook his head slowly. Then he said, "I guess I'll have to tell you the legend; my wife is too dumfounded to talk. About Machico — it was this way: it seems there were two lovers, Robert Machim and Anna d'Arfet. Some sort of Romeo-and-Juliet mix-up between their families, I suppose. Anyhow, they were fleeing from England to France. Their ship was caught in a storm and driven clear to the Madeiras. The place they were driven ashore was named *Machico* after them. I never heard whether they lived happily ever after, or were wrecked. But that's the legend."

Nat said, "Thank you. I'll tell her about it when I — " He felt his ears getting red. "My sister, I mean. She's always interested to hear about everything."

Mrs. Pintard was still dazed. "To the last fraction of — " Then, womanlike, she must have noticed Nat's flush. Her eyes danced. "Mr. Bowditch! You're sure it's your sister?"

"Are you trying to arrange a romance for my supercargo?" Captain Prince asked.

Nat laughed with them. He knew he might as well. A fine chance he'd have to make a girl fall in love with him. What was it Lizza had said to him once? "You *mathematician!* I wish you could at least pay compliments without arithmetic!"

CHAPTER 15

"SAIL, HO-O-O-O-O!"

That night as their boat took Nat and Captain Prince across Funchal Bay to the *Astrea*, Nat was still thinking about the legend of Machico. Maybe, he decided, before they weighed anchor, he'd write a letter to Elizabeth. There were several things he could tell her, about Lisbon, about the women who sold the fish, and about the legend of Machico. Or perhaps he'd keep that to tell her when he saw her. Perhaps he'd tell her about that, and then —

They boarded the *Astrea*. At the first glimpse of Collins' face, Nat knew something was wrong. Even before Collins spoke, Nat guessed that Lem was in trouble again. Nat had guessed right. For the third time, Lem Harvey was in the brig.

"That's the end of it!" Prince roared. "Hereafter,

someone else will drill the men at the guns!" He strode below.

Collins shook his head. "Now we will have trouble with Lem! Oh, for a good, rousing battle with a privateer! Or, better yet, a running fight — all the way to the Cape. That would keep Lem out of trouble."

"What's the matter with Lem, anyhow?" Nat asked.

Collins shrugged. "Lem was just born that way; born to fight. When he can't fight in a good cause, he just fights anyhow. There's no way to stop him. I could spread-eagle him, and give him three dozen lashes. He'd just swagger about his work with his back running blood."

Nat's stomach churned. "There ought to be some other way."

Collins raked him with a disgusted glance. "There isn't. Lem Harvey's born to trouble. He did pretty well while he was drilling the men; that let him work off part of his meanness. Now — heaven help us!"

The end of May they stood out from Madeira and headed south. Tom Owens took over drilling the men. Lem glowered and muttered under his breath. His sullenness seemed to hang over the whole crew. Nothing a man could put his finger on — but everything took twice as long to do as it should.

It was almost a relief one day when a sudden squall hit them and had the men fighting like demons to reef sails before the masts snapped. Something to struggle against seemed to clear the air. Was there no other way, Nat wondered, to keep the crew in a better frame of mind?

That evening after the storm Nat went to the fo'c'sle. The men hadn't dried out yet from the squall. Oilskins and jerseys hung everywhere; the stench of sweat and tar slapped Nat in the face as he entered the fo'c'sle.

A man who was talking stopped in midsentence. Eyes turned a sullen stare toward Nat.

Nat said, "Is there any man here who'd like to be master of a ship some day?"

From his mighty six-feet-three Lem Harvey looked down at Nat. When he spoke his words were respectful, but there was the undercurrent of a sneer in his voice. "Who wouldn't, sir? But what chance have we got, sir?"

"The same chance I had!" Nat barked. "In case you want to know, I stopped school when I was ten. I've been sailing by ash breeze ever since. What I've learned, I've picked up here and there, in my spare time. Now, between here and Manila, we're going to have some spare time. Does anyone want to learn some navigation?"

Tom Owens reached a calloused hand and almost broke Nat's fingers with his grip. "We're with you!" he said. "If you can get any navigation in our heads, good for you — sir!" He looked around him. "And if any man don't learn what he can learn, he — "

Lem Harvey stirred.

Tom Owens stopped, then went on lamely. "He — he — ought to be ashamed of himself."

Lem glowered. "You talking to me?"

Tom hesitated. He was a big fellow, but Lem towered over him. Tom mustered a grin, "I'm just talking for myself, Lem."

Lem stepped closer and stood nose to nose with Tom. "Just talking for yourself, eh? See that you remember that."

Nat said, "We'll begin tomorrow. Good night." He

returned to the deck and walked slowly aft. What had he done? Made more trouble? Well, whatever happened, he had started it, and he'd have to see it through.

Next day at four bells of the dog watch when the men gathered, Lem was not there. Nat thought to himself, Maybe he'll come around. He began, "Celestial navigation — or sailing by the sky — is what we'll talk about first. All of you know how — when we're close to shore — we figure our position by landmarks. And you know how — when we're out of sight of land — we figure our position by — well — we might call them *sky marks:* the stars, the sun, the moon . . . "

After a little, the men stirred restlessly. Nat felt someone behind him. Out of the corner of his eye he saw Lem Harvey glowering. Nat went on talking, trying to make a far-off star seem more important than Lem Harvey's nearby glare.

The weeks passed. Lem still glowered and muttered. But he was not affecting the crew with his mood now. They were standing a little straighter, and working a little more smartly. It did things to a man, Nat thought, to find out he had a brain.

Near the end of July the *Astrea* reached the Cape.

Johnny shivered. "Brrr! Mighty funny weather for July!"

Nat said, "It's winter at the Cape."

"In July, sir?"

"The weather's upside down," Nat told him. And with a cannon ball and a lantern, he showed Johnny how the earth goes around the sun. "You see, the axis of the earth, from the North to the South Pole, leans on a slant — like that. So, as the earth goes around the sun, first

the sun shines straight down on this part, and then on
that. Along about the end of June, the sun is shining
straight down up here — as far north as it ever does. So
north of the equator, where we live, it's the beginning
of summer. But down here, south of the equator, it's
the beginning of winter."

Johnny shivered again. "I hope it won't be this cold
all the way to Manila."

"It won't," Nat promised him. "After we double the
Cape, we'll be sailing toward the equator again."

Again the passage around the Cape of Good Hope
meant one long struggle against head winds. For three
days and nights the watches seemed endless, and the men
turned in all standing.

They left the storm behind and sailed north into the
Indian Ocean. "I'm glad that's over!" Johnny muttered.
Then, a bit glumly, he added, "But there's always some-
thing. I wonder what next?"

The "what next" was a warning cry from the lookout.
Nat was on watch when it came. "Sail ho-o-o-o-o-o! Off
the larboard bow!"

Lem did not wait for a command. He dashed forward
bellowing, "All hands on deck and man the guns!" Before the strange ship was close enough for the lookout to
see her colors, the guns were cast loose and ready for
action. But that was not fast enough for Lem. He roared,
"Get those matches lit!" And soon men stood ready,
blowing on the end of the long, slow-burning rope to
keep it lighted.

Captain Prince was on the quarter-deck with his spyglass.

Nat hailed the lookout. "What colors is she flying?"

The lookout had never seen the colors before. An ensign with the Union Jack, and red and white stripes.

"Some country ruled by England," Nat said.

Prince's laugh was a short bark. "It's the Flag of the East India Company, Mr. Bowditch."

Nat felt his face get hot. "Oh . . . I thought it was a country."

Prince shrugged. "You weren't so far wrong at that. There's many a nation without half as much power as the East India Company. They've held their charter almost two hundred years. When Queen Elizabeth gave it to them, she gave them enough power to hold their own against the Dutch. They've still got that power.

"They can take over land, wage war, and make peace. They've got their own ships, own uniforms, own flags. They've got a bigger and better-trained army than we ever had. When England got into this war with France, do you know what the East India Company did? They turned over a dozen frigates, well armed and fully manned — a dozen frigates!"

The ship of the East India Company did not seem interested in the *Astrea*. She held to her course and disappeared.

Lem bellowed, "Secure your guns!" He sounded disgusted.

At the sound of Lem's voice Captain Prince stared toward him. For the first time Nat remembered that Lem wasn't supposed to have charge of the guns. He saw Lem's jaws stiffen, his face grow sullen.

Nat spoke quickly. "Captain Prince, I ordered Lem to handle the guns. He was on my watch, and I — "

Captain Prince said, "I see . . . Send him aft."

Lem Harvey came.

Prince eyed him up and down. At last he spoke. "How did your men do? Were they fast enough?"

Lem's head jerked up. He grinned. "They were terrible, sir! Thumb-fingered fools, the lot of them!"

Captain Prince said, "Mr. Collins, have the men drilled twice a day until further orders. Have Lem and Tom divide the detail."

A smile twitched Collins' face. "Aye, aye, sir."

That night Nat was on deck after his watch, standing at the rail, watching the sky.

"Mr. Bowditch, sir?" a voice rumbled softly.

"Yes, Lem?"

"Begging your pardon, sir, but I didn't hear you order me to handle the guns this morning."

"Didn't you? I guess you were making so much noise yourself you couldn't hear anything."

"Aye, aye, sir." Lem shuffled his feet. "Mr. Bowditch, sir?"

"Yes, Lem?"

"I — I'm dumb. About book learning, I mean. Do you think you could teach me anything without — bawling me out?"

"Yes. But I couldn't teach you much as long as you bawled yourself out."

"Huh . . . sir?"

"I mean — suppose you made a little mistake — or didn't understand something right away. If you wasted my time cursing and yelling 'I can't get that! What's the use?' then I couldn't teach you."

"But — but — " For a long time Lem was silent.

Then he chuckled. "Mr. Bowditch, sir, heaven help you, but you've got yourself a job."

They shook hands on it.

Now, when Nat taught the rest of the crew, Lem stood listening. Whenever Nat and Lem had a spare minute, he taught Lem alone, so that he could catch up with the others. At first it was slow work. In spite of everything, Lem's anger would blaze at himself and he would storm and rage.

Time and again Nat said, "You're wasting time, Lem!"

Finally Lem settled down, and he learned so fast that he surprised even Nat.

The *Astrea* crowded sail now, moving north and east through pleasant weather. Then, so suddenly that it seemed to come between one watch and the next, the steamy heat of the tropics descended. The rigging went slack, tar melted and dripped, the wind died to fitful breezes. Men pumped endless buckets of water and carried them aloft to douse the sails so they would catch what little breeze blew.

Between his watches Nat worked over his notes to figure how to teach the men.

One night, near eight bells of the first watch, Johnny came to Nat's cabin, his teeth chattering with fright. "M-m-m-m-mr. Bowditch, sir, come quick! There's something wrong with the water! We're s-s-s-sailing into something!"

Nat hurried topside. All hands were on deck, standing in silent huddles. Nat went forward to the bow where Collins and Lem were staring into the water.

Johnny's teeth were still chattering. "The ocean's on f-fire. It'll b-b-burn us up!"

It was enough to frighten anyone, Nat admitted to himself. Where the bow of the *Astrea* cut the water, waves of white fire curled back. Captain Prince joined them forward. He stared at the water, too, and ordered a bucket lowered.

Lem bent on a rope, lowered a bucket, and pulled. The bucket rose from the water, rope, bail, and sides dripping white fire. Lem hesitated, swallowed hard, and brought the bucket up.

Captain Prince held a lantern close. The glow disappeared. He ordered the lantern covered, and once more the fire glowed. They leaned close to study the water. In the darkness they could see millions of tiny glowing specks dashing about in the water. "Phosphorescence," he said. He stood by the bow a moment, staring down at the curl of white fire. "What's your course, Mr. Collins?"

"Due east, sir."

"Very good." He turned and strode below.

Lem dumped the water overboard. A cascade of white fire streamed down. Eight bells came. The larboard watch lay below. The men of the starboard watch hesitated, shuffled their feet, then went to their posts.

Lem stalled around the longest. He cleared his throat. "Uh — Mr. Bowditch, sir? What did the captain mean? I mean — if you could think of something for me to tell the others. Some of them are scared, sir."

"You've seen fireflies, haven't you, Lem — lightning bugs?"

"Sure, Mr. Bowditch."

"These must be tiny sea animals that glow in the dark, like fireflies."

Lem released his breath in a long sigh. "Oh, sure. Like fireflies. I'll tell them, sir. Some of the poor fools are scared."

Toward six bells of Nat's watch, the water cleared. Lem swaggered aft. "All gone, ain't it? Too bad, sir. It was kind of pretty."

Nat's watch ended. He was below, and just dropping off to sleep when he heard the cry, "Land ho-o-o-o-o-o!" The lookout must have sighted Java Head. Nat rolled over and went to sleep. If the stories they had heard in Lisbon were true, they would all need rest before they faced the days ahead of them. They must beat their way between Java and Sumatra, fighting against the swift current of Sunda Strait.

The next day they stood off Java Head, waiting for a wind to favor them. Captain Prince was on deck, staring east toward Sunda Strait.

Johnny said, "Mr. Bowditch, sir, how do you sail against a current like that? Like they say it is in Sunda Strait?"

"A simple matter of mathematics, Johnny. If the current against you is flowing at — say — ten knots an hour, you have to be making at least eleven knots to move against it."

Captain Prince humphed. "A problem in navigation, Mr. Bowditch. And not so simple. We've got to tack off-shore where the wind can reach us. We'll be feeling our way with our lead. And we'll be fighting an uphill sea every mile of Sunda Strait."

The wind veered, freshened, and blew briskly. With

every sail spread and bellying taut, the *Astrea* moved
sluggishly against the current. Nat looked aloft into the
rigging, and found himself clenching his fists and holding his breath, trying to will more speed into his ship.

The wind slackened. The sails lost their taut curves.
The *Astrea* shuddered, stood still, and then began to
swing sideways in the current pouring like a mighty
river through the strait.

Nat jerked to attention and snapped orders. Men
dropped the anchors. Hour after hour crawled by, and
the waters clawed at the *Astrea,* trying to drive her back.
The sun rose to its zenith and poured down merciless
heat; afternoon came; then the sudden night of the
tropics swallowed them in blackness. But night brought
little relief from the heat. Men slumped on the deck
and tried to snatch sleep.

At four bells of the first watch the wind freshened.
Men leaped to the capstan and heaved the anchor. Slowly
the *Astrea* crawled forward, stopped again, and began to
swing sideways.

One day — two days — and three — they fought to
make headway. Sometimes they moved a mile before
they were forced to anchor again; sometimes only half a
mile; sometimes it seemed the huge dripping anchors
barely broke water before the wind died again. The
fourth day, when the *Astrea* lay at anchor, her sails limp,
another ship passed them, moving steadily against the
current.

Johnny was so angry he almost wept. "Look at that,
sir! Look! What's the matter with us? How can that
one pass us?"

"She's in ballast and riding high," Nat explained

wearily. "Her topsails and royals are catching a breeze that's too high for us."

After one week, the men were hollow-eyed, staggering with weariness. A smart breeze rose abaft the beam. They were almost too tired to cheer, but not too tired to get the *Astrea* under way in jig time. The wind increased. With every sail filled, the *Astrea* heeled over and moved smartly.

Johnny cheered. "Hooray! This time we make it!"

The wind veered sharply and threatened to drive them ashore. They fought to bring the *Astrea* far enough into the wind to keep her from going aground.

The wind died again. They anchored.

Lem Harvey glared down at Johnny. "When we're moving again — if we ever are — you open your mouth, and I'll keelhaul you!" Then he grinned. More and more often Lem topped off a roar with a grin. "Leastwise, I'll have a notion to."

Astrea II entering Manila Harbor

CHAPTER 16

A SIMPLE MATTER OF MATHEMATICS

On the evening of the tenth day they fought their way clear of Sunda Strait and anchored.

Prince called Nat to his cabin. He had a chart spread before him. "Well, Mr. Bowditch," he growled, "what do you think of the Dutch East Indies in general and Sunda Strait in particular?"

Nat looked at the chart. "I'm dumfounded," he admitted. "I've always thought of an island as — you know — small. I thought when we got to the East Indies we'd be just a stone's throw from anywhere in them. When it finally dawns on you — the size of them! Three thousand islands — over seven hundred thousand square miles — it's amazing, isn't it? Take Java, now. It looks small on a map, but it's several times as big as Massachusetts. A man certainly gets new ideas when he — "

Prince slapped his hands flat on the table, stood and

roared, "You *mathematician!* Is that all you have to say about Sunda Strait?"

"Oh . . . the Strait? I'd say it would be better to make your passage out in ballast. Just carry specie and buy your cargo in Manila. The higher we ride, the more chance we have of catching the wind. It's — "

Prince glared. "You say it's a 'simple matter of mathematics' and I'll brain you!" He sat down and studied the chart. "Now, to the next problem. Heaven knows how much we can depend on this chart. It's something over fifteen hundred miles to Manila. And what's between here and there . . ." He shrugged.

"At least we know the latitude and longitude of Manila," Nat said. "We can set our course for it as directly as . . ." He looked at the chart. "As directly as islands, straits, and reefs let us, can't we?"

Prince muttered something under his breath. "That's all, Mr. Bowditch."

On Saturday, the first of October, Nat went to Prince's cabin. "We should anchor in Manila Bay tomorrow, sir."

Prince stared at him long and hard. Suddenly he smiled. "That so, Mr. Bowditch? Manila tomorrow, eh? I'd better lay out my go-ashore clothes."

Nat shook his head. "I doubt if we'll need go-ashore clothes tomorrow, sir. I understand Manila Harbor's one of the biggest land-locked harbors in the world. More than seven hundred square miles. So we — "

Prince roared, "You —*mathematician!*"

Nat said, "Aye. aye, sir," and went topside. What in the name of sense, he wondered, had set Prince roaring that time? Manila Harbor was one of the biggest land-locked harbors in the world.

The next morning they were standing off Luzon. A pilot came aboard, sternly ordered all men out of the chains — no sounding of the harbor was allowed — and conducted them to their anchorage.

Nearby, another ship flew the stars and stripes. No sooner were they anchored than the ship hailed them, and the master, Captain Riddle, came aboard.

"From Salem, eh? Three cheers! You're the first Salem ship ever to enter Manila Harbor! How was it around the Horn?"

Prince said, "We came by the Cape and Sunda Strait. The Cape's not so bad — but I can't recommend Sunda Strait. We spent ten days getting through it — from the eighth to the seventeenth of September."

"You came from Sunda Strait since the seventeenth? In fifteen days?" Riddle asked. "Man alive, that's navigation!"

Captain Prince shrugged. "Not when you're sure of your longitude. Just a simple matter of mathematics. You . . ." He stopped, and glared at Nat.

"Captain Riddle, sir, have you ever seen a boat like this before?" Nat asked quickly, pointing to a canoe.

The three stood at the rail and watched the long, slim craft, carved from one log, with a huge sail woven of matting. The crew of eight dark-skinned, laughing natives looked as though they had not a care in the world.

"That canoe isn't big enough to carry a flying jib," Nat said. "But look at that sail! It must be a thousand square feet!"

"The canoe is an outrigger," said Captain Riddle. "See those bamboo logs athwart the boat, fore and aft, sticking out over the water, with the other logs joining their ends?"

"Yes, but I thought that must be cargo — something too big to get into the canoe. You mean they're fastened on the canoe?" Nat asked incredulously. "They're — "

A sudden gust of wind caught the huge sail, and the canoe heeled over, throwing up a spray of water.

"There she goes!" Nat yelled.

But six of the laughing brown men slid out on the bamboo logs on the windward side, and their weight balanced the huge sail against the pressure of the wind. The canoe righted itself and sped through the water.

Captain Prince pursed his lips in a silent whistle.

"That's something I'll tell — " Nat stopped, as Prince looked at him.

Several times during their weeks at Manila Nat felt Captain Prince's thoughtful stare on the back of his neck. In December, when they weighed anchor for home, the captain drawled, "Well, Mr. Bowditch, you'll have a lot to tell her — your sister, I mean — won't you?"

"Aye, aye, sir." And Nat remembered something he had to see about right away.

What was Elizabeth doing now, he wondered, half-way around the world? That night he began to jot notes of all he would tell her — and what he would leave out. The earthquake in Manila — he'd better skip that — or should he? Would she hear about it from someone else and be worried?

Week after week, as he stood his watches and taught the crew with one part of his mind, another part of it seemed busy checking off the miles — and the months — between him and Elizabeth.

At dawn one February morning, when they were in the Indian Ocean, the lookout's cry gave warning, "Sail ho-o-o-o-o-o! On the starboard bow!"

On the heels of the cry came Lem's bellow, "Loose your guns!"

Long before the ship was near enough for the lookout to see her colors, the *Astrea* was ready for action.

When the lookout yelled, "She's American!" Lem Harvey growled, "Secure your guns!"

The ship was the *Stanley,* from Boston, Captain Daniels commanding. Captain Daniels gave them news of home. Grim news. America was at war with France. Not declared yet, he said, when he sailed, but doubtless it was declared by now. The French were sinking American ships left and right.

"Keep your guns shotted and your powder dry!" Those were the parting words he bellowed through his trumpet.

From then on, Nat could feel the tension in the air. He knew the lookouts strained their eyes as never before, sweeping the horizon for an enemy sail. He knew that many a man turned in all standing, ready for instant action. He knew he slept with one ear cocked for the pell-mell thud of feet overhead, and the cry, "All hands on deck!"

It was the middle of a peaceful dog watch when danger struck. There was not a sail on the horizon, or a storm cloud in the sky; just a fair wind abaft the beam and the *Astrea* reaching for the Cape. Tom Owens stumbled up a companionway yelling, "We've sprung a leak!"

Lem Harvey was the first man at the pumps.

Nat heard him growl, "Why couldn't it have been

something simple — like a fight!" He knew what Lem
meant. A bad leak was something you couldn't conquer
with a broadside from your guns. Even if it didn't drive
them to a long delay in a foreign port, it would be with
them every league of the way to Salem Harbor. They'd
be short-handed at all other work. Men would be
needed at the pumps, night and day.

As the weeks passed, they held their own against the
leak — but no more. At last they loaded the deep-sea
lead, sounded — and brought up black mud! They were
off Block Island!

"We'll make it!" Tom Owens roared.

Lem growled, "There's many a reef between Block
and Baker's Island!"

But the *Astrea* plowed on. Sand in the deep-sea lead
now. They were off Nantucket.

Tom grinned. "How about it, Lem?"

"I'd like a dollar for every ship that's gone aground
between here and Baker's Island," Lem growled.

At dawn one morning late in May came the lookout's,
"Land ho-o-o-o-o!" They had sighted Cape Ann. The
thought flicked through Nat's head, They're too tired to
cheer. I know I am. Then a hoarse roar split the air and
fairly shook the rigging, and Nat found he was yelling,
too.

Captain Prince was on deck now, grim-jawed, alert.
Danger was not over when they sighted Cape Ann. Still
six hours ahead of them, at the speed they were making.
Six hours, and one miscalculation could wreck a ship in
sight of home.

Gales Ledge to starboard . . . Pilgrim Ledge . . . how
many ships had been wrecked within a stone's throw of

home . . . Whaleback to starboard . . . A good berth now to the northwest point of Baker's Island . . . Midchannel now between Baker's Island and Little Misery . . . Captain Prince was keeping Naugus Head and Coney Island in line now . . . a narrow lane of safety . . . Hardy's Rocks and Rising States Ledge and the shoals of Eagle Island on the south; on the north, Bowditch Ledge.

When he was young, Nat remembered, he had felt proud of a ledge named Bowditch. Later he learned that having a ledge named for you or your ship meant disaster instead of honor.

Bowditch Ledge astern to the north of them . . .

Thoughts of home filled Nat's head, mixed with his thoughts of the channel they were following. Was Dr. Bentley on his lookout now? Had he sighted the *Astrea*? Was his flag whipping in the breeze, giving the news to the town? West by north now, to give a good berth to the Haste . . . Was Elizabeth on the captain's walk, watching for the *Astrea*? What was she thinking about? Was she remembering their good-by? Or had she forgotten? Nat could feel his heart pounding. Over the roar of blood in his ears, he heard Prince's voice, "Southwest by south."

The helmsman answered, "Aye, aye, sir; southwest by south."

Abbot Rock to starboard now . . . The shoals of Middle Ground to larboard . . . Would Elizabeth be on the wharf when they anchored? Of course she wouldn't, Nat told himself. He'd rather she wouldn't be. All that crowd and confusion . . . everyone talking at the same time . . . wives greeting their husbands . . . mothers looking for their sons . . . Every Tom, Dick, and Harry there, wanting to know about his venture. She wouldn't be there . . .

Elizabeth was the first person he saw when he reached the wharf . . . Elizabeth, standing on something to see over the crowd, and smiling and waving. Somehow he wormed his way through the crowd to reach her.

"Nat!" Elizabeth called. "We've been waiting for *hours!*"

A man's voice said, "Seems like *days!*"

Nat saw the man with her then — a tall, handsome chap, with dark hair sweeping back in a widow's peak and smiling dark eyes.

The young man said, "I don't suppose you remember me, Mr. Bowditch. I haven't been around Salem much for years. I was knee high to a grasshopper when I went to Harvard."

Nat shook hands and smiled and called David Farrel by name. He said of course he remembered him, it was fine to see him again.

"It's good to see you, too, sir!" David told him. "Elizabeth talks so much about you. Like you were her big brother — or something. Almost like you were her father!"

Of course, Nat thought. He should have known. She was seventeen. He was twenty-four. Just a simple matter of mathematics, Mr. Bowditch! he told himself grimly. You should have figured that one out!

CHAPTER 17

LUNARS AND MOONLIGHT

"I want to hear all about everything, Nat," Elizabeth said.

David Farrel smiled. "We both do!"

Nat thanked them. He told Elizabeth he'd try to see her soon. When I get over feeling like a fool! he told himself. Just now, he said, he must go to the Custom House with Captain Prince.

"Perhaps this evening?" Elizabeth asked.

It might be a week or two before he could see her, he said. He'd be awfully busy, taking care of the cargo.

For a moment Elizabeth's eyes studied him gravely, then she smiled, and said it was fine he was home. She left the wharf — with David Farrel.

After Captain Prince and Nat reported to the Custom House, they went to Mr. Derby's office.

Mr. Derby questioned them briefly, and nodded. His mind did not seem to be on the success of the *Astrea*. He told them news of the war threat. The trouble with France dragged on.

"It'll never be settled until this country wakes up and builds a navy!" Prince said.

Mr. Derby nodded. "President Washington knows we need a navy." He unfolded a newspaper. "Here's what he said in his Eighth Annual Message to Congress, last December." He read some passages he had marked:

"To an active external Commerce, the protection of a Naval force is indispensable . . .

. . . it is in our experience that the most sincere Neutrality is not a sufficient guard against the depredations of Nations at War. To secure respect to a Neutral Flag, requires a Naval force, organized, and ready to vindicate it from insult or aggression. This may even prevent the necessity of going to War."

Prince said, "And he's right! But when will he convince Congress?"

"They're finally convinced," Mr. Derby said. "They've authorized the building of six frigates."

"Humph!" Prince said, "*six* frigates!"

Mr. Derby nodded. "I know, it is not enough. I'm urging the government to let private citizens build warships, too. Salem will build a frigate, the minute we have permission."

Nat thought of what men said of Mr. Derby — that he could "see around corners." Did he see war coming now, in spite of all our efforts to stay at peace?

Mr. Derby's secretary interrupted to say that Mr. Blunt, the publisher from Newbury, wanted to see them.

A moment later an impatient young man entered the office, nodded briefly to Mr. Derby and Captain Prince, and glared at Nat.

"I was talking to Mr. Collins," he said. "He tells me you think you found an error in Moore's *Navigation!*"

"I did."

"In which table?" Nat told him. Mr. Blunt gave a short laugh and relaxed. "Do you know who compiled that table? Nevil Maskelyne! The royal astronomer of England! You'd be as apt to find a mistake in — well — in Newton's *Principia!*"

"*Principia?*" Nat said. "I did find an error in it. Let's see if I can quote the spot . . . Well, roughly translated, it went something like this . . ." And he quoted the passage and pointed out the error.

Mr. Blunt's jaw fell. "Well, I'll be . . . Where did you go to college? London? Paris? You didn't get that kind of education here! Where did you go?"

"I didn't."

Mr. Blunt opened his mouth twice before any sound came. Finally he said, "Er — could you point out the error in Maskelyne's table?"

"Which one?" Nat asked. "There were several."

Mr. Blunt's round face swelled and turned red. At last he swallowed hard and muttered, "All of them."

Captain Prince said, "And you might ask him about his new way of working lunars, Mr. Blunt."

"A new way of working lunars!"

Nat explained it briefly.

Mr. Blunt's jaw dropped again. "But — but — that's tremendous! I'd like to include it in the new edition of

Moore that I'm bringing out. And — and — if you could just cast your eye over some of the tables in the book . . ."

"You don't 'cast your eye' over navigation tables!" Nat barked. "When I checked that one table of Maskelyne's, I worked every figure three times, just to be sure I was right!"

"Three times? Every figure? But why in — "

"Why not?" Nat roared. "Mathematics is nothing if it isn't correct! Men's lives depend on those figures!"

Mr. Blunt swelled up and turned red again, but after a little he said, "Quite so, Mr. Bowditch. I wish we had time for you to check all the tables in Moore. At any rate, I certainly want to include your new method of taking lunars."

Nat promised to see him in two weeks, when they'd taken care of their cargo. Soon he, Captain Prince, and Mr. Derby were deep in figures.

Time and again during the next two weeks Nat thought of Elizabeth. Was he ready to see her now? Ready to feel like a big brother — or father — or something of the sort? He'd give himself a little more time, he decided.

When he was done checking on the cargo, he was glad he had another excuse to put off seeing her. He must talk to Mr. Blunt about Moore's *Navigator*.

"I wish we had time for you to check all the tables," Mr. Blunt repeated. "But a great many of the signatures of the book are already printed." He must have seen Nat's bewilderment. He said, "Perhaps you think of a signature as a man's name. We printers have another meaning for it. A signature is a single large sheet of paper, on which certain pages of the book are printed. We arrange the pages so that, when the signature is folded and trimmed, the pages are in order."

Nat said he'd be glad to check some of the tables that weren't yet printed. Glad of an excuse to keep busy, he thought.

He worked on the tables, and the thought of Elizabeth stayed somewhere under the figures — most of the time. I'm getting over it, he told himself. But every time there was a knock on his door, his heart jumped. Maybe it was a message from Elizabeth. But it never was.

Dr. Prince came to see him. "I just wanted to remind you, Nat — the Philosophical Library is still open to you — if you want to read the books."

Nat thanked him. "I've been thinking about the library, Dr. Prince. I'd like to join it now — if it's all right with the members."

"More than all right! We'll be honored to have you!" Dr. Prince's eyes twinkled. "I'm sure the books will be pleased. No one else has ever understood them so well as you."

Dr. Holyoke came, wanting to hear all about the lunars, firsthand, and to talk astronomy with Nat. Nat felt a warm glow of pleasure. Dr. Holyoke was more than a beloved physician; he was one of the founders of the American Academy of Arts and Sciences in Boston.

"I correspond with quite a few astronomers," Dr. Holyoke said, "but I don't have much chance to talk to one."

"I'm no astronomer!" Nat protested.

The Captain's Walk

"No? But you figured an easier and more accurate way to check longitude. Astronomers and scientists have been working on that quite a while — for several hundred years."

"The chronometer's the best way," Nat said. "When all ships can afford a chronometer . . ."

"Until they can, they'll bless you and your lunars — even if you aren't an astronomer. Come to think of it — I believe a carpenter invented the chronometer, didn't he?" Dr. Holyoke grinned and was gone.

Alone again, Nat tried to work, but it was no use. He really should call on the Boardmans, he told himself. He should tell Mrs. Boardman about the man he'd met in Manila who'd known her husband.

At the Boardmans', old Minna greeted Nat with a smile. Mrs. Boardman and the girls would be so sorry to miss him, she said. They were in Boston. Hard to tell when they would be back. Mrs. Boardman wrote that they were having a fine time. So many parties. David Farrel was in Boston, too.

Nat went back to his work.

Autumn came; the trees flamed scarlet and yellow; the harvest moon was gold. A note came for Nat. In Elizabeth's handwriting. His fingers shook when he opened it. A group were going Thursday night to a farm for a party, Elizabeth wrote.

> The grownups will visit in Mr. Wiggins' house, but we're going to have a party in the barn. A husking bee. And bob for apples, and everything. I do hope you can come. Especially.

Nat went to sleep smiling. She wanted him — especially!

Thursday morning, he saw David Farrel. David was cheerful, too. "We're awfully glad you can come, Nat. I — well, this is just between us — but I'm hoping to make a very important announcement tonight."

"Are you?" Nat realized how flat his words sounded. He forced himself to smile. "That's fine!"

"Nothing settled yet," David said, "so you won't tell anyone?"

"Not a word," Nat promised. He went home with a cold lump in his chest where his heart should be. So that was why Elizabeth hoped he could come — especially. He was to be "among the first to know." "Big brother!" Nat muttered. "It's a wonder David didn't ask my permission instead of her mother's!" Five times that afternoon he decided he wouldn't go. Five times he changed his mind.

At seven o'clock that evening he was alone in the crowd in Wiggins' barn. Not that anyone could tell how he felt. He was sure of that. He knew his face kept smiling, all by itself; he'd given it a good talking-to before he came. He knew his tongue kept making the right answers. But his thoughts were anywhere else — everywhere else. The party at Mary's, when he'd first talked to Elizabeth; the morning after Lizza's funeral, when Elizabeth had brought him the Latin book; most of all, the morning he sailed on the *Astrea*, when Elizabeth told him good-by. When Elizabeth stood on tiptoe . . .

The crowd began husking corn. David called cheerily, "Here, Nat! Sit by us! We've saved you a place!"

Nat's face smiled; his tongue said, "Oh, fine!"

He sat by Elizabeth, husked corn, and smiled at David's constant stream of chatter.

"I haven't found a red ear yet!" David complained. "I should have bribed Mr. Wiggins to save me a dozen." He bent his head and looked into Elizabeth's face. "You know what that means, me proud beauty! Thirteen kisses!"

"A dozen is twelve," Elizabeth said. "Tell him, Nat."

David laughed. "I have a baker somewhere in my ancestors. I always give thirteen kisses for a dozen. One for your right eyebrow, one for your left eyebrow, and — "

Nat didn't realize his hands had stopped husking corn. An ear hit him on the chin. Someone yelled, "Nat! Get to work!"

Smiling again, Nat grabbed an ear of corn, ripped back the husk — the ear was red.

A shout of laughter went up. "Kiss her, Nat! Kiss her!"

Nat's heart sank. What a time to kiss Elizabeth. He'd dreamed of this minute halfway around the world. In his dreams, they would have been alone — maybe looking at the stars. He would have told her the legend of Machico and then — somehow — he'd never figured out just how — he would have worked around to telling her that he loved her.

But now, in the midst of two dozen teasing, laughing people, he must kiss her and make a joke of it. He ordered his face to smile again, and put his arm around her. He couldn't think of anything funny to say, so he borrowed David's words. "Come here, me proud beauty!"

She turned to him, laughing, and was suddenly grave. "Nat!" she whispered.

Nat found he didn't have to work around to what he wanted to say. He just said it. "I love you, Elizabeth. I've always loved you since you were . . ." And he kissed her.

Another ear of corn hit Nat. Another voice shouted, "Here, Nat!"

Nat saw the ripped-back husk, and the red kernels. He laughed and tossed the ear on the pile of corn. "Keep it! I don't need it!" He pulled Elizabeth to her feet. "Where's your mother?"

Elizabeth's eyes widened. "In . . . in . . . the house."

"Then come on! I have something to say to her!"

Outside the barn, Elizabeth stopped, and leaned against the barn door. "Let's just stand here a minute, Nat, till I — get my breath."

Nat chuckled, leaned his hand against the door, and stood watching her face in the moonlight.

"Is — is — the moon that big everywhere, Nat?"

"Nowhere but in Salem," he told her. "Other places, it's just — well — moon-size."

"How — how — big is moon-size?"

He teased her. "You really want to know? Or are you scared of your mother?"

"I'm not a bit scared! I want to know about the moon!"

"Well," Nat drawled, "the closest estimation we have is that the diameter is two thousand, one hundred and sixty miles. Now, shall we go?"

From the doorway, someone said, "People are right. Figures *do* run out his ears, don't they?" It was Polly. The three of them laughed together.

"She's just stalling; I think she's scared of her mother," Nat said.

"Pooh! Aunt Mary won't argue about it," Polly said. "She should have seen this coming for ages!"

Nat blinked. "What!"

"A woman can always tell about things like this."

Nat teased her. "A *woman?*"

Polly tossed her head. "A *girl,* then! But a girl knows more about love before she's a woman than a man ever knows!" She went back in the barn.

Elizabeth said, "Tell me some more about the moon, Nat."

Nat chuckled. "The radiance of the moon is special in Salem. It comes from your face." He stopped, pleased with himself. "That was almost like poetry, wasn't it? I — I — wish I could make pretty speeches."

Elizabeth tucked her hand under his arm. "Pretty speeches! When a man can make pretty speeches, I always wonder how long he's been practicing! Come on, Nat. Let's tell mother!"

In March, just before Nat's birthday, they were married. The months that followed were the happiest Nat had ever known. The only shadow that ever crossed their days came from news of the sea; a ship long overdue, a ship returning with word of missing men, a ship reported lost in action against the French, and men coming back with grim tales of storms off the Cape or the Horn.

Then Elizabeth's eyes would darken with fear. "Nat.

I hope you never double the Cape again! I — I — couldn't sleep, thinking about it!"

"The Cape's not so bad. You're safer there than lots of places. For instance — take the Mediterranean. There — you'd be running from a French privateer, and probably be hulled by a Barbary pirate." And he told her horrendous tales of what happened to crews that were captured by the Barbary pirates — men put in chains — sold as slaves.

Elizabeth finally agreed that perhaps the Cape wasn't so bad, after all. Nat felt proud of himself, making the Mediterranean sound worse than the Cape.

Captain Prince came to call. The *Astrea* was sailing again in August. "I want you as supercargo, Nat. And — no more second mate's duty for you — no watches to stand."

Nat grinned. "I'd want to be worth my salt between ports."

"You are; *you* and your teaching. I've spent a long time at sea, but I've never had less trouble with a crew. So you'll come? Supercargo — and all your time your own between ports?"

"Now?" Elizabeth protested, "when there's so much trouble with France?"

Prince shrugged it off. "There's nothing to worry about. Do you think Derby would send the *Astrea* now if he thought there was any danger? He knows things are quieting down."

Elizabeth didn't look convinced. "With all those frigates being built? The *Constitution* and the *Constellation* and — "

"That's why things are quieting down," Prince declared. "The best way to stay at peace is to be prepared for war."

Elizabeth finally smiled. "Of course. I'll remember that. And I — I — hope you have a good voyage."

Prince smiled. "You're a proper mariner's wife, Elizabeth. You know an anchor won't hold if the cable's too short. A man always needs another shot in the locker."

Elizabeth's smile was puzzled.

"Another length of cable to stick out when a ship threatens to drag her anchor," Prince said.

"I'll remember that," Elizabeth promised.

"Good!" Captain Prince smiled. "Nothing to worry about. This is just a short trip. To Cadiz — then into the Mediterranean, to Alicante." He waved a gay salute and was gone.

Into the Mediterranean! Elizabeth paled and was silent. Nat couldn't think of anything to say, either — not after all the stories he'd told her about the dangers of the Mediterranean. She said she had just thought of something, and fled up the stairs. Nat started after her, and then turned back, cursing himself for a fool. What could a man tell a woman about the sea — so that she wouldn't worry?

Elizabeth did not come downstairs again until suppertime. She was still pale, but she laughed and talked of everything but the sea. After supper, though, conversation lagged. Nat was glad when someone knocked. It was Lem Harvey, dressed in his best, with his wife and his brother-in-law, Zack Selby.

"The wife just had to see you, Mr. Bowditch, sir."

Amanda Harvey said, "To thank you for what you did for Lem! I — I — can't tell you how much I thank you!

My Lem's signed on the *Betsy* as second mate!"

Zack Selby sneered. "You'd think he was running a whole fleet of ships, single-handed, to hear her take on."

Sour grapes, Nat thought. Zack's still before the mast, and he's ten years older than Lem. He said, "I'm glad for Lem, Amanda, but I didn't do it for him. He did it for himself. He worked and studied harder than any man in the crew."

"That's just it, sir!" Amanda said. "Nobody else ever got him to stick his nose in a book!"

Zack sneered again. "Books! Salem men have come to a pretty pass when they have to sail by books! Time was they could double the Horn with nothing but log, lead, and lookout."

"That's right," Nat agreed. "They doubled the Horn. And sometimes they got home again. But what about all the ships that don't come home? If 'sailing by book' makes men a little safer, what's wrong with it?"

Zack lowered his gaze and shuffled his feet. "Ain't just my idea," he muttered. "Plenty men think what I think. Sailing by book is a mighty lubberly business."

Amanda said, "Oh, *you!* Don't pay any attention to him, Mr. Bowditch! His nose is out of joint. Lem and me — we're mighty proud of a book-sailor in the Harvey family!"

When they had gone, Elizabeth smiled. "And I'm mighty proud of a supercargo in the Bowditch family. Nat, darling, forgive me for being such a coward this afternoon. I won't do it again, I promise you."

Two days later, Captain Prince was back — not smiling this time. "You and your teaching!" he roared. "Lem Harvey's shipped as second mate on the *Betsy!*"

Elizabeth's eyes widened. "But, Captain Prince, aren't you proud of him?"

Prince flushed, then growled, "Oh, of course! Just pleased to pieces. But — but — blast it all — he was the best man we had on the guns! We needed him!" And he stamped out.

Elizabeth gasped. "Nat! There is danger! He knows it! Oh, darling . . ." She stopped. "I'm sorry. I'm not going to spoil the rest of our time together."

Nat hugged her. "Ten years from now, we'll be laughing at this, won't we?"

"Of course! No more solemn talk!"

She kept her promise until the August morning the *Astrea* was to sail. Then she stared at Nat with stricken eyes. "Nat, dear . . . Good-by, darling."

Nat teased her gently. "I'm going to teach you French. They say it better: *au revoir*. That's till your return. Good-by always sounds so final."

Elizabeth whitened. "I didn't mean it that way, Nat! I didn't! But — if it were good-by, Nat, remember this. You've made me happier than any other girl ever was in the world!"

A chill tingled Nat's spine. He kissed her. *"Au revoir."*

"Good-by, Nat . . ." Then, quickly, she added. "I'll learn French when you come back!"

Nat smiled, but he felt a cold lump in his chest.

CHAPTER 18

THE *ASTREA* TO THE RESCUE

When Nat went aboard the *Astrea,* two sailors handled his gear for him, staggering under the weight of an extra sea chest.

Mr. Collins said, "What have we here, Mr. Bowditch? A private store of cannon balls?"

"Books and charts," Nat told him. "I'm starting now to check every figure in every table that's published. Just to see how many errors are in them."

Collins stared. "Man, that'll take you a year!"

"I'll be lucky if it doesn't take three years."

"But why in the name of sense should you slave over — "

Nat bellowed, "Because they ought to be right! That's why!" He started for the companionway. Someone in ducks and a striped jersey grinned and saluted. For a moment Nat didn't recognize him. "Johnny!"

Johnny swaggered. "Johnny Gorman, able seaman, sir!"

"Congratulations!" Nat told him. He hoped Prince wouldn't feel too bad about the loss of a cabin boy. He was going to feel bad enough about the loss of Lem. He went below, stowed his gear, and returned to the deck. Tom Owens was busy at one of the guns. Maybe Tom would console Prince about the loss of Lem; Tom was a mighty handy man, too, with the guns.

Once more the crew froze to attention; once more Captain Prince came on board, and whipped that stern glance around, seeing everything, looking at no one.

It's just his go-to-sea face, I guess, Nat decided. He probably won't smile between here and Cadiz.

Nat was right; he didn't.

A month later Spain loomed on the horizon. A blockade of British ships stood between the *Astrea* and the harbor of Cadiz. Captain Prince answered the hail of a British ship, ordered his longboat overside, and he and Nat went to present their papers to the British captain.

The Englishman scanned their papers, asked dozens of questions, and gave them a pass to enter Cadiz and trade. "Watch out for French spies," he told them. "They're everywhere. We even found a Frenchman in one of our crews, with a plot to blow up our powder room. Luckily, his pronunciation gave him away."

"The way he'd say — well — for instance, 'commencement'?" And Nat gave the word its French pronunciation.

The British captain raised his eyebrows. "Exactly. You mean, you speak French?" He looked at Prince.

"Congratulations, sir, on having an educated man on board. Not the usual thing on a — a — merchant ship, you know."

Prince's eyes glinted. He was probably thinking that what the Englishman almost said was, "Not the usual thing on an American ship." He drawled, "Yes, an educated man is handy. For instance — when there are errors in Moore, he can find them."

"Errors in Moore!" The Englishman stared.

"Not really Moore's fault," Prince said soothingly. "The mistakes were in one of Maskelyne's tables." And he returned to the *Astrea* looking very pleased with himself. "Mr. Collins, call the men aft — down to the last one — even the cabin boy!"

The men gathered. Little Charlie Waldo, the new cabin boy, listened big-eyed while Prince explained the danger of French spies. "Mr. Bowditch will tell you how you can spot them by their accent. Keep your ears cocked. If a man with that accent wants to come aboard for any reason — call Mr. Bowditch."

As Nat explained, he watched Charlie's face. I'll bet, he thought, Charlie finds himself a spy before we leave Cadiz.

The next day when they anchored off Cadiz the health officers came aboard. Nat saw Charlie edging around, his head cocked, listening. Then something jerked Nat's attention from Charlie. The Spanish officer picked up their logbook in one gloved hand, wheeled, and tossed it overboard.

Nat roared at him in Spanish. The health officer smiled and explained. They always dumped logbooks overboard. Didn't the señor know that salt water would purify the book and banish disease? They fished up the book, dripping wet, scanned it, and bowed to Nat. Everything was in order and safe. The *Astrea* could trade with Cadiz.

That night Nat smiled when he wrote to Elizabeth about the salt-water cure for their logbook. He was glad when he had things like that to tell her.

The next night, after he had visited Cadiz, he had things he could tell her, too — about the city of stone, built on a rocky promontory, jutting out into the blue sea.

They must whitewash every building every year. Everything is so white that the glare hurts your eyes. The streets are so narrow, and the buildings so tall that you feel hemmed in when you walk here. No wonder they have such tall buildings, though. They have nowhere to go but *up*.

He stopped writing, and stared at the paper. When would Elizabeth get this letter, he wondered? No chance to send it back to her, unless they hailed a ship coming from the Mediterranean, going back to America. Maybe he'd just have to carry it home, and they'd read it together. When he got home . . . Nat sighed. Already the time seemed long. He laid his letter aside and went on deck for a walk before he turned in.

Charlie Waldo was on deck, talking to himself.

"Good for you, Charlie," Nat said, "you have that French accent, all right. You won't miss them if they come prowling around, will you?"

Charlie smiled, and bent his head to wipe his wrist

over one cheek. In the moonlight Nat could see the youngster's tearstained face. Poor tad, he was homesick.

"Charlie, I wonder if you could do something for me?"

"Aye, aye, sir!"

"I'm working on a problem in navigation. I'd like to explain it to you. If I can make you understand, I'll know I've got it."

"Aye, aye, sir! Anything to help!"

They walked the deck while Nat explained. Charlie was quick. He got the explanation much faster than grown men generally did.

"Thank you, Charlie. That's helped."

"Thank you, Mr. Bowditch, sir. You don't know, but you helped me, too!" Charlie grinned and went below, still muttering his words with the misplaced accent.

One morning during their second week in Cadiz, when Nat was in Prince's cabin, Charlie came to them, goggle-eyed. "We've got him, sir! A French spy! I can tell by the way he talks!"

Captain Prince's mouth twitched. "Come, Mr. Bowditch." They went on deck. Charlie was right. The erect, soldiery-looking man did have a French accent.

He was Count Mallevant, he told them — once of the French navy. He had fled to Spain during the French Revolution. Nat knew that Charlie's sigh of disappointment came from his heels.

Count Mallevant said, "I understand there is a scholar aboard this American ship — who is interested in astronomy. A very great scholar who has discovered a new way to work lunars."

Prince nodded toward Nat. "There's your very great scholar — Nathaniel Bowditch."

Mallevant invited Nat to visit the new observatory at Cadiz.

When the count had gone, Prince bowed solemnly. "How-do-you-do, scholar."

Nat laughed, but he felt the same warm flood of happiness he had felt when Dr. Holyoke called him an astronomer. He couldn't explain how he felt to a grown man, though — what it was to remember when he was twelve and found he'd never go to school again. *Nathaniel Bowditch — indentured.* He shrugged off the memory.

That night, when he stood in the observatory, he wished that he could tell Elizabeth what it was like to be there — looking through the telescope that seemed to bring the moon and stars close enough to touch. It was late when he returned to the *Astrea,* but he wrote to her. "You seemed very near when I looked at the moon. Because I knew you could see it, too." He smiled at that sentence, pleased. Maybe he'd learn to say things the way he wanted to some day!

"All hands on deck!" He heard the yell and jumped to his feet. Dimly he realized he'd been hearing the boom of cannon in the distance. He hurried topside. The gunfire was coming from the British fleet. What had happened? Was Napoleon attacking? He was supposed to be somewhere in the Mediterranean.

The deck of the *Astrea* was alive with action — men running to secure battle lanterns — to loosen the guns. Presently a boat approached them and a British officer came on board. He was smiling and almost too excited to talk.

"Nelson has trounced Napoleon's fleet! In the mouth of the Nile! We've got him now! Bottled up in Africa!"

So it was just a celebration. Tom Owens growled, "Secure your guns!" Nat smiled at the words. Tom sounded as disgusted as Lem Harvey would have been.

The Englishman said again, "Bottled up in Africa! No more trouble with Napoleon . . . I hope."

"What about the French privateers in the Mediterranean?" Prince asked. "We're standing out of Cadiz for Alicante soon."

"Into the Mediterranean? You'll be safer in convoy with our fleet."

So the *Astrea*, and some four hundred other vessels, started in a vast convoy, guarded by British warships. It was not long before the lookout on the *Astrea* saw three small vessels dropping astern.

Collins leveled his glass. The lagging vessels were American. "What are the fools up to?" he muttered.

Prince studied them, too. "They're too heavy laden to keep up. Scuppers under — the lot of them. Serve them right if . . . " Then he said, "Bring her about, Mr. Collins."

"Aye, aye, sir."

There was no hesitation from the first mate, or from any of the crew as they fell to with a will, to bring the *Astrea* about. They left the protection of the convoy and headed back toward the floundering little vessels. When the *Astrea* was close enough to speak the ships, Captain Prince hailed them. The *Astrea*, he told them, had nineteen guns, and a crew that could use them. Cheers rose from the little ships.

Tom Owens swaggered and grinned. "One-man convoy! That's what we are!" Nat smiled to himself. Lem Harvey wasn't the only man "born for a fight."

For two days the *Astrea* trimmed sail to the speed of the floundering vessels. Tom began muttering under his breath. What was the use, he wanted to know, wallowing along with fools who didn't know how to sail? "They couldn't make six knots in a trade wind!" he grumbled. "They don't deserve —"

The lookout's singsong, "Sail ho-o-o-o-o-o!" froze every man in his tracks.

Then, with a glad bellow, Tom leaped for the guns.

Captain Prince came on deck and leveled his glass. "Three of them," he said, "and flying French colors."

There was no doubt about the colors — or the intentions — of the three ships. They were altering their course, bearing straight down on the *Astrea*. When the decks were cleared, the guns bowsed out, Prince went below with Nat.

Prince opened the logbook and picked up a quill. "Better note this now," he said dryly. "May be a little rushed later." He made the entry and dusted the ink with sand. "We'll need someone in the powder room when things start," he said.

Nat sat down and pulled off his shoes. He knew the danger of a scuffed nail's striking a spark and setting off the powder. "I can take care of the powder room."

Prince frowned and started to speak. Then he shrugged. "Why not? I was going to say we can't risk having our navigator blown to bits. You know, if the powder room gets a direct hit — it goes. But if the powder room's blown to bits, the *Astrea* won't need a navigator, will she? Carry on, Mr. Bowditch." He went topside.

Nat went to the powder room, blinking in the gloom.

The only light there came from a small round window into the next cabin. For a moment Nat was disappointed. He'd thought of getting a little work done while he waited. He'd forgotten they couldn't risk candles or lanterns near the kegs and bags of powder.

Johnny was there, sloshing down the floor with water. "They say it helps some. Of course, if that tier of kegs got a direct hit . . . " He shrugged and grinned. "Good luck, Mr. Bowditch, sir!"

Nat's eyes grew accustomed to the dim glow. It really wasn't too dark, he decided. And no use just sitting there twiddling his thumbs till they needed him to hand up powder. He went to his cabin and got his slate and pencil.

The next thing he heard was Prince's bellow. He started and jumped to his feet. "Aye, aye, sir! You ready for powder?"

Prince said, "The Frenchies didn't like our guns. They got close enough for a good look, then crowded sail and cleared out. Tom's disgusted. Sorry I forgot about you and left you down here so long."

"Long?"

"Great guns, man, you've been here three hours!"

"You're sure, sir?"

Prince broke out in a roar of laughter that brought Collins below. Prince told him the joke. "I give up! I've been through a lot in my day, but I never before saw a man huddle on a powder keg and forget where he was for three hours. That's one for your letter to Elizabeth!"

Nat shook his head. "She might worry, sir."

"Take my advice and tell her," Collins said. "You're married a long time, you know. And women always hear everything, sooner or later. If you skip anything, some kind friend is sure to say, 'Did your husband ever tell you about the time . . . ' So you tell her first — the way you want her to hear it."

Your husband . . . Nat smiled at the sound of that. He closed the powder room and dogged shut the door, and went for his shoes. In his cabin, he returned to his work. Nothing for him to do now until Alicante.

They had been off Alicante about a week when a ship flying the American flag anchored near them — the *Ember,* from Salem, Captain Gorman commanding. Nat hadn't realized how glad he'd be to see someone from home until Captain Gorman came on board the *Astrea.*

Captain Gorman did not seem half so glad to see Nat. He nodded abruptly and said, "Captain Prince, I'd like to see you below."

Nat felt his temper rising, but he shrugged off his anger. Captain Gorman probably had something on his mind. He'd be in a better mood after he had talked to Captain Prince.

Charlie came to him, frowning with importance. "The captain's compliments, Mr. Bowditch. He'll see you below."

When Nat entered the cabin, Prince said, "Sit down, Nat, sit down, boy."

Captain Gorman sat with head bowed, his elbows on his knees, staring at nothing. Prince strode up and down the cabin a few turns. "I'm — I'm not going to stand off and on about this, Nat. Elizabeth — your wife — is dead."

Captain Gorman said, "That's all I know, Mr. Bowditch. A ship passed me that had left Salem later than we had. They gave me the word."

Nat didn't know when they went out. He realized finally that he was alone and the cabin was growing dark. Eight bells sounded. He had offered to take the anchor watch. He went topside.

Mr. Collins said, "You've been relieved, Mr. Bowditch."

Nat thanked him and went forward to the bow. For a long time he stood there, staring at the sky. The moon rose and made a glittering path on the water. Nat found himself staring down into the water. How deep was it, he wondered . . .

Charlie Waldo spoke at his elbow. "Mr. Bowditch, sir?"

Nat stiffened. "Yes? What is it?"

"I need you, sir. Could you help me, please? This navigation I'm trying to learn . . . "

"Of course, Charlie. Come along to my cabin." For an hour he worked with Charlie over the problem that had stumped him — explaining this way and that, until the boy understood.

"I have it now, sir! Thank you!"

"Thank you, Charlie Waldo. You may not know, but you've helped me, too."

He went topside again, and found Mr. Collins. "I'll stand the next anchor watch," he said. "I don't seem particularly sleepy."

Collins nodded. "Right, Mr. Bowditch." He was silent for a moment; then he went on quietly, "I remember when I lost my wife. Work helped."

CHAPTER 19

STRANGE SAILING ORDERS

Nat thought he had learned to face his sorrow, until they sighted Cape Ann and he knew that in a few hours he would be home. His hands began to shake. Desperately he tried to keep his mind on the rocks and shoals of the entrance to Salem Harbor. Gales Ledge to starboard . . . Pilgrim Ledge . . .

What could he say to Elizabeth's mother?

Whaleback to starboard now . . . and a good berth to the northwest point of Baker's Island . . .

What was there to say that wouldn't sound hollow and empty?

Midchannel now between Baker's Island and Little Misery. Nat stared toward Naugus Head and Coney Island. Must keep them in line . . .

If only he had a way with words he could give her some comfort!

Hardy's Rocks on the south . . . the Rising States Ledge

. . . the shoals of Eagle Island. On the north, Bowditch Ledge . . .

Elizabeth's mother would probably hate the sight of him. He'd only remind her of the happy months last summer, before he had sailed.

"I'll tell her I want to return Elizabeth's dowry — leave everything just as it is. I'll say I have to stay with the ship while we unload the cargo. I'll get out. That will make it easier for her."

Captain Prince's voice said, "Southwest by south."

They were almost there. Soon Abbot's Rock to starboard . . .

Almost home! Nat drew a quivering breath.

When they had anchored, Captain Prince said, "Go along, Mr. Bowditch. You aren't needed here."

"Aye, aye, sir." Nat left the ship.

Polly was waiting on Derby Wharf. She stretched out both hands to him and kissed his cheek. "Dear Nat. Aunt Mary's so anxious to see you. I came to meet you. I thought if I told you about Elizabeth it would be easier."

"You're like what Lizza used to say of *her,* Polly. You have eyes in the back of your heart."

Polly shook her head quickly and winked back tears. "I'm not a bit like Elizabeth. But I loved her. And — I'm like Aunt Mary. I love you, too, because you made Elizabeth so happy."

They walked slowly home, and she told him of Elizabeth. It had been consumption. "It takes more people than the sea, doesn't it, Nat? I wonder if doctors will ever find a way to conquer it — the way they are conquering smallpox?"

Mrs. Boardman was waiting for him. "It's good to have you home, Nat. I've missed you."

The lump of dread in his heart went away. It was not until after supper, when he climbed the stairs, that the awful aloneness hit him. He turned toward the big corner room where he had said good-by to Elizabeth. He stood by the closed door, unable to open it.

Polly came up the stairs with a lighted lamp. "I've fixed the east bedroom for you, Nat. Sort of like a study — with a desk and all."

Nat followed her to the room — saw the bookcases, the big desk, the armchair he had liked. He said again, "You do have eyes in the back of your heart."

Three men from the *Astrea* tramped up the stairs, bringing his gear.

Polly whispered, "I sent for your things." She called, "In here, please!"

The men looked around the room and nodded. They declared it was a proper berth for Mr. Bowditch — him with his tables of figures, long as main to bowline. They tramped down the stairs again.

Polly said, "I hope you have something to work on — hard."

"Why are you both so good to me?"

"Pure selfishness," Polly told him. "We like to have you here."

It was more than a week later before Nat got around to what he had wanted to tell Elizabeth's mother — about returning the dowry. "We had such a short time together. I don't deserve to keep anything."

Mrs. Boardman said, "You proud, foolish *man!* I never want to hear another word about it!" She seemed to think she had settled that and went on talking about something else.

Dr. Bentley brought Nat up to date on the news of Salem. Mr. Derby was broken in health — dying — but he had accomplished that last dream of his — to have Salem build a frigate for the United States Navy. He had advanced ten thousand dollars of the seventy-six thousand needed. Dr. Bentley showed Nat a copy of the broadside that had been printed to announce the building of the ship:

THE SALEM FRIGATE
TAKE NOTICE:

Ye Sons of Freedom! All true lovers of the Liberty of your country! Step forth and give your assistance in building the Frigate to oppose French insolence and piracy. Let every man in possession of a White Oak Tree be ambitious to be foremost in hurrying down the timber to Salem, and fill the complement wanting, where the noble structure is to be fabricated, to maintain your rights upon the Seas, and make the name of America respected among the nations of the world. Your largest and longest trees are wanted, and the arms of them for Knees and Rising Timber. Four trees are wanted for the Keel, which all together will measure 146 feet in length, and hew 16 inches square.

Polly went with Nat, Dr. Bentley, and Captain Prince to see the Salem frigate in the ways.

Dr. Bentley stared at the hull that was taking shape. "Elias Hasket Derby's last dream," he said. "Free men of Salem, building a ship to defend America."

"We're going to need it some day," Prince said. "Mr. Derby knew. That man always could see around corners."

They went to the Derby wharf. A strange crew was aboard the *Astrea,* making ready to sail. Some men in Boston had bought the ship. Captain Prince watched the crew. "Lubbers; I wouldn't sail with that crew if they gave me the ship!"

Nat spoke before he thought. "I would. Right now I'd sail on anything, to anywhere. I'd . . . " He stopped, embarrassed.

Captain Prince and Dr. Bentley were embarrassed for him. They began to talk about something else.

Polly looked squarely into his eyes. "I know you would. I don't blame you."

Bless Polly, she did understand. She knew that friends and neighbors — even old friends and good neighbors — couldn't fill the emptiness in his heart.

When he and Polly reached home there was a letter waiting for Nat. He had been elected a Fellow of the American Academy of Arts and Sciences! It seemed to Nat his mind fumbled, trying to grasp the meaning, as cold fingers fumble, trying to untie a knot.

"Nat! How wonderful!" Mrs. Boardman said. "I — I — must see Mary Crowninshield! I just remembered something . . . " And she put on her bonnet and hurried out.

Polly's eyes twinkled. "Salem will know about this before dark, from Gallow's Hill to the Beverly landing!" Then she sobered. "I wish it had come sooner, Nat." She did not say more; she did not need to.

In the days that followed she had fun bringing Nat

reports of Salem's reaction to the news. Not everyone knew what it was all about — but they were sure it was fine. Science? They knew Nat had worked out something about navigation. Was that science? Navigation was just navigation, wasn't it? Getting your ship there and back? It didn't take a scientist to do that, did it? Scientists were bearded men who read heavy books and talked big words, weren't they? Who ever heard of a scientist going to sea?

Captain Prince came around one evening. "Did you mean what you said, Nat — that you'd sail anywhere on anything?"

"Yes, I did."

"Then you'll get your wish. The new owners of the *Astrea* want us to go as master and supercargo — to Batavia, for coffee." He smiled grimly. "They assure me I can pick up a better crew in Boston than the one we saw handling the ship."

Nat said, "At least they'll be better — when you get done with them."

"Most of our men are scattered, but I did see Charlie Waldo."

Nat grinned. "Fine; it's always a help to have a handy cabin boy."

Prince stood. "Then you'll go? I'll write them tonight. We'd better drive to Boston when the time comes. The stage might not have room for all your gear."

Hab and William both were in port before Nat left for Boston. Tanned, brawny fellows that they were, they teased Nat, asking him how he kept his feet in a squall. But their teasing was mixed with respect. They had been hearing tales from men who had sailed under him.

The night before their ships sailed again, Hab and William came to supper in the Boardman home, and filled the room with their laughter and tall tales.

"Did Nat ever tell you about the time he worked problems on a powder keg?"

Mrs. Boardman said, "Dear me! I hope the keg was empty!"

Hab chuckled. "Not much it wasn't! The little runt was sitting right in the middle of the powder room! For three solid hours!"

"Nathaniel!" Mrs. Boardman gasped. "I hope I never hear of your doing anything like that again!"

Polly's brown eyes danced. "You won't," she said, "unless someone tells on him."

After supper, Mr. Blunt came to call. He was about to bring out another edition of Moore, he said. Would Nat go over the whole book — if he had time — his next voyage — and check it for errors?

Nat said he intended to do that very thing.

Mr. Blunt beamed. "Good! I'll consider it a personal favor!"

"It's no personal favor to you — or to any publisher!" Nat barked. "I'm doing it for the men who depend on it when they sail!"

Mr. Blunt's famous temper started rising. His face swelled and turned red. But he swallowed hard. "Quite so, Mr. Bowditch. Quite so."

When Mr. Blunt had gone, Hab grinned and shook his head. "William, the little runt has a temper!"

William smiled at Nat. "Only about things that matter."

They took Nat with them to see Mary and Lois. Mary

smiled at them lovingly. "I'm so proud of you — all three of you! Sit down — and let me just *look* at you! It's been so long since we were all together!"

They talked until the birds began a sleepy twitter.

William looked out the door. "Hab! It's almost daylight!"

"Come on!" Hab bellowed, "or we'll be making a pierhead jump!"

So the good-bys were brief. It was better that way, Nat thought. He wished his good-bys could be as short when he'd leave for Boston. They wouldn't be. He'd leave Salem with Captain Prince. The master of a vessel didn't have to make a pier-head jump. Everything waited for him.

If only he didn't have to say good-by to anyone. Especially to Polly. Young girls were always the worst of it, he told himself. The night before he and Captain Prince were to leave, he spent the evening with Mary and Lois. He'd be in a hurry tomorrow, he told himself. That would cut short the good-bys.

When he returned to his room late, there was a note on his desk from Polly. She had had to go to Danvers — she said.

> . . . I suppose I should say I'm sorry to miss telling you good-by, but I'm not. I don't think much of good-bys, do you? Have a good journey! . . .

Blast that girl! Nat crushed the note, hurled it on the floor, then picked it up, smoothed it, and put it away in a book.

He was still muttering to himself when he and Captain Prince started to drive to Boston. Captain Prince gave him a sidelong glance. "A little shy of ballast, aren't you, Mr. Bowditch? A crank little vessel this morning."

Nat did not answer.

At last they reached Boston and drove to the wharf. They went aboard the *Astrea,* and found her deserted of all but a watchman. Such a crew, he complained. Not the first crew — the second one. The owners had advanced a month's wages to the men, to clear their debts. They'd brought them on board, and fed them well. Then the scoundrels had jumped ship.

"Good riddance," Prince said.

They went to see the owners, and met the first and second mates. Mr. Cheevers, the first mate — slim, hard-bitten — looked capable enough, but bad-tempered. Mr. Towsen, the second mate, had his berth at the request of one of the owners.

We're probably supposed to "make a man of him," Nat thought.

The owners, too, apologized about the crew. They'd had no idea the men would jump ship, or they'd have taken precautions.

"Good riddance," Prince said again. "We'll find a better lot."

But when they had scoured the waterfront boarding-houses, Prince shook his head over their scourings. They picked the best of the lot, advanced a month's wages to settle their debts, and signed them on. The men came aboard — some walking — some being dragged.

By evening the crew was aboard, and the *Astrea* was cleared to sail. Nothing to do now but wait for the tide.

Captain Prince said, "Mr. Cheevers, how soon can you get under way?"

Mr. Cheevers was so astounded that he stuttered, "You — you're — the tide — "

"Mr. Cheevers!"

"Aye, aye, sir!" Mr. Cheevers gave orders.

A baffled, bewildered crew blundered on deck, and walked round the capstan.

"Hove short, sir," Mr. Cheevers reported.

"Set jib and mainsail, Mr. Cheevers."

"Aye, aye, sir."

Prince watched in grim silence while the men fumbled with the sails. Then he said, "Break her out, Mr. Cheevers!"

And the *Astrea* was under way.

Nat saw the sidelong glances Mr. Cheevers shot toward the captain. He could read Mr. Cheevers' thought — Are we sailing with a madman?

Presently, Captain Prince said, "So, Mr. Cheevers. Ready with your anchors."

More bewildered than ever, Mr. Cheevers shouted orders. The *Astrea* came to again, and anchored. Captain Prince cast a look over the long way back toward the shore. "Call your men aft, Mr. Cheevers."

Nat had heard Prince talk to his crews three times, but he had never heard anything like this talk. Prince finished by advising them not to jump ship, since they were hardly in condition to swim that far. With that, Prince turned on his heel and went below.

Now the meaning of the strange sailing time dawned on the crew. Nat looked at Mr. Cheevers and saw anger, amusement, and respect in his eyes. But the faces of the men before the mast were frightening to watch. Not two of the lot, Nat figured, had had the slightest intention of sailing on the *Astrea*. They had doubtless heard of the clever desertion of the other crew. They'd planned the same stunt, signed on for a square meal and a month's pay. Now they faced months at sea — the terrors of the Cape — the grilling passage through Sunda Strait — a layover in Batavia — where men died like flies.

The baffled rage was naked on their faces.

Charlie Waldo approached Nat. "The captain's compliments, Mr. Bowditch. He'll see you below."

Captain Prince said nothing about the scene on deck. He was not even wearing his grim go-to-sea look. He spoke softly, with a drawl. "We'll stand anchor watch tonight, Mr. Bowditch, along with our crew. So they won't get lonesome. If we get past tonight with a full crew, they won't have another chance to jump ship till the Cape. After tonight we can rest easy."

We can rest easy . . . With a dozen men who probably hated the sight of their captain? With a dozen landlubbers whose only recommendation for the sea was that they had failed on land? Nat wondered.

CHAPTER 20

BOOK SAILING

A month later they had weathered the Roaring Forties of the North Atlantic. The crew had begun
to be sailors. The last poor lubber had got his sea legs.
Fingers that had bled on the halyards were healed, and
black with tar. Every man could hand, reef, and steer.
They could loose the guns and get ready for action; not
so smartly by half as the crew Lem Harvey had trained
— but they could do it.

The *Astrea* was her old self again. Dingy decks were
holystoned white, and the rigging was taut, tarred, and
dressed in its chafing gear.

But a sullen mood hung over the ship, like an evil mist
over a swamp. Even when he was below deck, in his
cabin working, Nat could feel hatred staring at the back
of his neck, as though an animal stalked him in the night.

Lupe was the worst of the crew, because he smiled. A

slim, swarthy young fellow, Lupe moved softly as a cat, and purred when he spoke.

"We can rest easy," Prince had said, "until the Cape."

Nat wondered what Prince would say if he knew how his supercargo felt about Lupe — that it wasn't quite safe to turn your back on him. Was it imagination, Nat wondered, or was Lupe always watching him? Did Lupe follow him at night when he was on deck taking sights? For two weeks now, he had had that feeling of someone behind him. Twice, when he'd been standing on deck in the darkness, he'd swung about quickly, as though searching for a star in another direction. But he had seen no one.

Though tonight promised to be a good one for taking a lunar, Nat worked stubbornly at his checking of Moore's tables. Once he thought he heard his door open. He started, wheeled, and broke out in a cold sweat. This had to stop! He slammed Moore's book shut, picked up his sextant and slate, and went topside. Deliberately, he went forward, beyond the waist of the ship, and stood at the larboard rail, facing the water. I'll stand here, he told himself, till I get over being a fool!

He didn't know how long he'd been standing there when he felt, rather than heard, cat-soft movement behind him.

A voice purred, "Señor?"

Nat forced himself to turn slowly. "Yes, Lupe?"

Lupe's teeth flashed white. He held out one brown hand. Across the palm lay a knife. "Do not stop me, what I say, señor. I say it quick, or I lose the nerve. Two weeks — maybe three — I try to get up the nerve."

So Lupe had been following him. Nat said again, "Yes, Lupe?"

"I want to ask you, señor — could we trade the — the — know-how?"

"The know-how?"

"I want to learn the — the — navigation. I teach you to throw the knife — you teach me the navigation, eh?"

Nat began to laugh, then stopped suddenly when he saw the smile stiffen on Lupe's face. "Forgive me, Lupe. But the idea of my learning to throw a knife — it just struck me funny."

"But you could, señor! And it is a good thing to know! Also, I teach you to sing the *serenatas!*"

Nat only smiled this time. "That's funnier still — me singing a serenade."

"No, no! señor! You could do it! Then you win any señorita in the world! First — the knife! Your rivals — *pouf!* They are gone! Then the *serenata.* Ahhh! The lady — she is yours! You want to get married, don't you, señor?"

"I was married, Lupe. My wife — is dead."

Lupe's smile vanished. His eyes widened. "You win the lady? No *serenata?*"

"No *serenata.*"

"Por Díos! How you do it?"

This time Nat didn't even try to stop laughing. "It's all right, Lupe. I'll be glad to teach you navigation. Tell me — how much mathematics do you know?"

"The — the — numbers?" Lupe's smile flashed again. "Very quick! I count on my fingers! Add-up! Take-off! That's good, eh?"

"Well, it's a start," Nat admitted. "Addition and subtraction come first."

"Then you teach me?"

"Er — what else do you know about numbers?"

Lupe's smile faded again. "Just add-up, take-off, señor. There is more? I cannot learn the navigation?"

"Addition and subtraction . . . Let me think, Lupe . . ." Nat took a turn on deck. "If we had logarithmic tables of all the trigometric functions, you could work any problem in navigation with nothing but addition and subtraction."

"Log tables? I make them," Lupe promised, "with the wood!"

"No, no, Lupe. They aren't that kind of tables. These tables are just lists of numbers. I could figure them out, all right . . ."

"You do that, señor? For Lupe?"

"On one condition," Nat promised.

"Anything, señor! I teach you magnificent *serenatas!* You have the world at your feet! You can't fail!"

"Is that how you won your wife, Lupe? With serenades?"

Lupe sighed. "No, señor. She not marry Lupe. Her brothers — they are first mates. They say she cannot marry Lupe. Cannot marry a man before the mast."

Nat took another turn on deck until he was sure he could keep from smiling. He faced Lupe again. "I'll teach you on one condition, Lupe — that all the foc's'le studies with you."

"Por Díos! But why?"

"Because it's easier to teach a dozen men than one man. How about it, Lupe? You think you can persuade them?"

For a moment Lupe frowned. Then his slow smile stretched again. He looked at his knife. He purred, "Yes, señor. They do it. They do anything for Lupe." He prowled away and disappeared in the shadows.

The next day, during the dog watch, Nat began. The men worked hard; Lupe saw to that. But Nat worked harder. The tables he figured now were longer "than main to bowline." And explanations that had worked for other crews were still too hard for these men to grasp. So they worked — across the equator, to the Cape, and into the Indian Ocean they slaved — Nat and the men before the mast.

Mr. Towsen, the petulant second mate, came to Nat's cabin one night. "Mr. Bowditch, just what are you doing with the foc's'le?"

"Teaching them navigation."

Mr. Towsen's lip curled. "How much can they learn?"

Nat laid aside Moore, and spread the logarithmic tables he was making. "When these are done, every man of them will be able to work a lunar."

Mr. Towsen flushed, then whitened. "What kind of discipline will you have on this ship? Teaching the hands something your officers can't do?"

"No reason you can't learn it, too," Nat told him. "You're just as bright as Lupe — I think. Now, if you'll excuse me . . . "

Mr. Towsen stamped out. Nat went back to checking Moore's tables. At last he muttered in disgust, slammed the book shut, and went to Prince's cabin. "I'm through with Moore! Do you know how many errors I've found — so far? Eight thousand!"

Prince stared. He said it was impossible.

"I can prove it, point by point! Do you want me to get my figures and — "

Captain Prince said *no* — with trimmings. He'd take Mr. Bowditch's word for it. "So, Mr. Bowditch, what now?"

"I'm going to write a book of my own. And it's going to have three things these books don't have. First, the tables will be correct! Second, every sea term, every maneuver, everything a man needs to know, will be explained in words any able seaman can understand. Third, I'll put in tables — so that any seaman can solve problems in navigation — even if he has to count on his fingers to add!"

Captain Prince thought it was the wildest idea he'd ever heard. He said so — with more trimmings. "Even if you could do it — which I doubt — it would take you the rest of your life — if you lived that long!"

"I can do it," Nat roared. "I'm doing it now! If I can teach Lupe to take a lunar, I can do anything!" He stopped. Silence echoed in the cabin. He'd been yelling again.

Captain Prince stared at him for a count of ten. "Carry on, Mr. Bowditch."

"Aye, aye, sir." Nat went topside. Tonight was going to be a good time to start teaching the foc's'le to take lunar observations.

By the time the *Astrea* reached Sunda Strait, Nat had made good his threat to Mr. Towsen. He had taught the crew to take lunars, and Mr. Towsen too. The second mate had fought the idea like a harpooned whale, but he had had to learn, in self-defense.

Shooting the sun

When they anchored off Batavia, Nat stretched and grinned with relief. They had sailed with a sorry crew and arrived with able seamen — with very able seamen! Smiling, he went ashore with Captain Prince and Mr. Cheevers to bargain for their cargo of coffee.

Two days later the three men stared at each other. There was no coffee to be had.

A British captain gloated over them, and made polite sounds of sympathy. "Too bad — your voyage for nothing. An expensive mistake. If you'd sailed with a cargo, you could sell that. But — you sailed in ballast, didn't you? Nothing but specie. And now — nothing to buy. Really too bad."

Captain Prince said there was always Manila.

The British captain looked even more pleased and sounded more sympathetic. "The monsoons, my dear fellow. Perhaps you don't know about them? Steady as the trade winds — excepting that they do vary with the seasons. Just now, if you tried to make Manila, you'd be sailing in the teeth of the northeast monsoon all the way. One doesn't sail to Manila this time of year. It just isn't done."

They returned to the *Astrea,* a grim trio. Charlie felt their mood as they sat down to mess. Dishes rattled when he served them.

"Too bad," Mr. Cheevers said, "that our trip has failed."

Nat banged his fist on the table. "It hasn't failed! We can still go to Manila!"

Mr. Cheevers lifted an eyebrow. "Fighting head winds all the way? That, my fine-*figured* friend, would take some navigating!"

Nat snapped, "So we navigate it!"

Prince stiffened. His eyes narrowed. His glance flicked from Mr. Cheevers to Nat and back again. "Mr. Cheevers, how soon can we be ready to sail? To Manila?"

Again Mr. Cheevers stared at his captain and stuttered, "But — but — sir — the head winds — "

"*Mr. Cheevers!*"

"Aye, aye, sir!" With a wild look in his eyes, Mr. Cheevers went on deck.

Nat scrawled a quick note to Polly and sent it to a ship that was weighing anchor for home. They were going on to Manila, he told her, so they'd be a little longer getting home. A good trip so far. A fine crew. He smiled a little as he wrote that. But, after all, they were a fine crew now, weren't they?

On deck that night Charlie approached Nat. "Mr. Bowditch, sir — the monsoon — it's blowing the wrong way now?"

"Yes, Charlie."

"And we'll be — uh — tacking against the wind? Zigzagging back and forth? Like we did for a little while, coming around the Cape?"

"Yes."

"All the way to Manila?"

"All the way."

"We — we'll do it all right, sir?"

"Of course," Nat told him. "It's a simple matter of — We'll do it, all right."

Day after day the *Astrea* moved in a crazy zigzag. Once she'd sailed from Sunda Strait to Manila in fifteen days. No making it in fifteen days this time. December ended;

January came and passed; February began. Eight long weeks out of Batavia the *Astrea* anchored in Manila Harbor.

The *Phoebe,* from Boston, was anchored nearby. Her master, Captain Hudson, came on board the *Astrea* to ask news of home. "And how was it around the Horn?"

"We came by the Cape," Prince told him. "Stopped in Batavia; no coffee there, so we came on to Manila."

Captain Hudson stared. "Not in the teeth of the monsoon?"

Prince shrugged in an offhand way. "Why not?"

"But — but — no f — I mean, no man — "

Prince smiled. *"No fool tries to sail in the teeth of the monsoon?* Is that what you meant?"

"Well, yes," Hudson admitted. "I mean — the navigation. You'd have to have a man who could work lunars — "

Prince shrugged again. "What's so hard about lunars? Every man in my crew can work a lunar."

Hudson's face was blank. Then he laughed, "Come on, tell me. How did you do it? Just sheer blind luck?"

Prince said, "I'm not joking. Ask any man on board."

Charlie, who was nearby, straightened and cleared his throat.

Prince nodded. "Go ahead, Charlie. Tell Captain Hudson how you calculate a lunar."

"Aye, aye, sir!" Charlie stiffened, stared straight ahead and rattled off the formula. "That's the way we do it, sir. It's better than waiting for the moon to oc-cult a star." He looked at the bewildered Captain Hudson. He added helpfully. *"Oc-cult —* that means *cover up,* sir."

Captain Prince had a sudden coughing spell.

A British ship hailed the *Astrea*. Captain Willoughby came aboard. He, too, wanted to know how it was around the Horn.

Captain Hudson began to enjoy himself. "They just arrived from Batavia. Yes, we know it isn't done, but they did it."

Captain Willoughby searched their faces, as though trying to figure out the joke. "You mean you have a man who can work lunars?"

Captain Hudson laughed. "One man? They have a crew that can work lunars! The cabin boy just explained it to me! I tell you, Captain Willoughby, there's more knowledge of navigation on this American ship than there has ever been before in the whole of Manila Bay!"

From across the deck, Lupe lifted his hand in a salute to Nat. His grin flashed white in his swarthy face. A smile danced in his eyes. Nat grinned back at him. A good man, Lupe.

Captain Hudson grinned at Charlie and said he wished he could stay around a while to study with him, but he was just about to up anchor and clear for home. Nat scrawled another note to Polly and sent it by the *Phoebe*. They'd be a little longer getting home than he had thought when they left Batavia, he told her. A little delay on the trip to Manila. But everything was fine. They should make it home by September, if all went well.

It was September when they sailed smartly into Boston Harbor, every man an old salt, the *Astrea* stripped of her chafing gear and gleaming with fresh paint and varnish.

When they paid off the crew, Lupe reached a calloused hand to wring Nat's fingers. "Señor, you are one guy!

Ever you sail again, you send for Lupe, eh?"

"I doubt if I will," Nat told him. "I think I've swallowed the anchor."

Two weeks later, Captain Prince and Nat were on the road home. The first people they saw in Salem were Amanda Harvey and her brother Zack. Nat hailed them, stopped the horses, and got out to greet Amanda. "What's the news from Lem — your book sailor, Amanda?"

Amanda began to cry, and Zack hurled a string of curses. Book sailing had cost Lem's life. The *Betsy* had gone aground — because of book sailing. "Talk to Tim Yates," he sneered. "He's the only one that survived. He'll tell you about book sailing! Come on, Amanda!" He grabbed her arm, and shoved the sobbing woman along the street.

Nat got the story from Tim Yates when they reached Essex. Tim did not rage as Zack did. But what he said cut almost deeper. A mistake in Moore had wrecked the *Betsy*.

"It seems Moore had figured 1800 was a Leap Year. So he had the calculations for the moon off. Seems like an awful little mistake in a book makes a big mistake in miles. That's what I heard the mate say when we was trying to get off the reef. I don't understand much about it. Don't want to, I guess. You see, Mr. Bowditch, if he hadn't been depending on the book, he'd have been sounding. Log, lead, and lookout. That's the way to sail. We depended on the book, though. So we went aground. When we saw we couldn't get off, and we was going to break up, we tried to run the boats in, we did — through the surf. But it was dark as the hold in a storm. We couldn't watch out for rollers. We couldn't see the rocks. When I come around, I was the only one there."

Nat said, "You'd have been safer heading straight out from shore."

"Yeah," Tim agreed. "I guess that ought to be in a book, too." Then he flushed. "I didn't mean that like it sounded, Mr. Bowditch. But — but — a book ain't no good. I wonder if that's what happened to your brothers, too? Book sailing?"

Nat wet his lips. "My brothers?"

Hab and William had both been lost, Tim told him. He said again he was sorry, and shuffled off.

CHAPTER 21

"SEALING IS SAFER"

Stunned with the news, Nat went to see Mary and Lois. Lois wept, but Mary was beyond tears. She only said, over and over, "I hate the sea, Nat. I hate it. *I hate it.*"

When she asked him what he was going to do now, he only said he hadn't decided. It was no time to tell Mary he was going to write a book on navigation. It was no time to talk to anyone in Salem about book sailing — not right now.

Mrs. Boardman was glad to see him. Polly was not there. Mrs. Boardman hoped she would come for a visit soon. She missed Polly.

In his bedroom-study, Nat began to work on his tables, checking and rechecking every figure. When he had worked so long that the numbers danced in front of his eyes, he switched to other parts of the book. Over and over again he wrote each paragraph, each sentence, to explain navigation to the man before the mast.

As he worked, he remembered the men he had trained: Keeler — Johnny — Owens — Lem ... When he thought of Lem he stopped working and pounded his fist on the desk in helpless rage. Then he thought of Hab and William, and memories drove him back to his work until the pain was numb again.

Mrs. Boardman worried about him. "Nat, dear, you should get more rest!"

"I'll rest when the book is done."

Mrs. Boardman had no answer when he spoke of the book. She only sighed and shook her head. Polly came from Danvers to see her Aunt Mary. Mrs. Boardman said, "Thank goodness you've come! Now someone will help me scold Nat!"

"What's he doing?"

"Working too hard. You'd think he was writing a whole cyclopaedia instead of just one book."

Polly's eyes widened. "A book? What about?"

Nat was getting edgy about the book. "Navigation!" he snapped. "Is there any reason why not?"

Mrs. Boardman gasped, but Polly seemed undisturbed. "About time you did one. Come on and tell me about it."

They talked until supper, and after.

The next day at dinner Mrs. Boardman said, "Nat, you worked till all hours last night."

"It was going well," Nat said, "after talking to Polly. I suppose it's the long line of sea captains in her blood."

Polly nodded. "Cut my teeth on a marline-spike," she

declared, "and tied knots instead of playing with dolls, I did."

Mrs. Boardman looked reproachful. "Polly! You're not going to be a bit of help to me! I tell you, he's working too hard."

Polly stopped smiling. "Aunt Mary, think of it this way; if a ship was aground off Salem Harbor — say on Rising States Ledge — or the Haste — every able-bodied man in Salem would be out there trying to save the crew, wouldn't he?"

"Of course!"

"And the women wouldn't try to stop them, would they? No matter how long and hard they worked? No matter if they were risking their lives?"

"No-o-o-o," Mrs. Boardman admitted, "when a ship is in danger, men do everything they can."

"Well, every ship is in danger, every time it sails," Polly said. "But the more men know about navigation, the safer our ships will be, won't they? Nat isn't working to save just one ship. He's working to make every ship safer every time it goes to sea. Every ship in America!" Polly was really warming to her idea. "Every ship in the world!"

"Polly, dear!" Mrs. Boardman smiled. "You don't expect other countries to pay attention to an American book, do you?"

"Why not?" Polly wanted to know. "Nat's the best teacher of navigation in the world. And that isn't my say-so. It's what Father says. He's had men who've sailed with Nat. He said, 'When it comes to teaching any fool navigation, Nat Bowditch is the . . .'" She stopped and rolled her eyes at her aunt. "Well, you know how Father talks. But what he meant was that Nat can teach navigation."

Mrs. Boardman shook her head and looked at Nat's plate. "He isn't eating a thing."

Polly looked at his plate, too. "If you don't want any dessert" — she nodded toward the door — "then get along back to work."

Nat chuckled, excused himself, and raced up the stairs. The rest of that day, and that night, the work went faster than it ever had.

He had no idea what time it was when someone tapped on his door. It was Polly with a tray of cookies and milk.

"I'm not a bit hungry," he declared.

"Then don't eat it." She set the tray on his desk. "Happy figuring! Good night!" And she was gone.

Nat went on working. After a while something bothered him. His hand was pawing at the empty tray, fishing for another cooky. "Now when did I . . ." He shook his head. "That Polly!"

After that, he found himself listening for her step. When he heard her coming, he would lay aside his work, lean back, and twiddle his thumbs. "Sit down a while, Polly. I'm just at a stopping place."

One night two weeks later, Polly set the tray down and turned to the door. "I'm busy tonight," she said. "And tomorrow night, you'll have to raid the galley for your own lunch."

Nat felt a quick stab of disappointment. How silly, he told himself. He followed her to the hall. "You're going to a party?" He smiled. "Have a good time."

"I'm going home," Polly said. "I just came for a little visit. Aunt Mary gets lonesome, and I — "

"But — but — you can't go, Polly! What would I do without you? To talk to? To laugh with? You can't ever leave me, Polly! You — " And she was in his arms. "I love you, Polly."

"I've always loved you," she whispered. "Ever since I can remember."

"Polly, will you . . ." He stopped. They stared at each other. He knew they were thinking of the same thing.

Polly said it. "But what would Aunt Mary say? How would she feel about — "

A door opened, and Polly's Aunt Mary said, "She's happy for both of you. That's how she feels about it." She kissed them. "I'm going to ask you to do just one thing for me. Live here — with me. You're like my own children. I'd miss you so."

In late October, when the leaves were a riot of red and gold, they were married.

Mrs. Boardman said, "Nat, I hope you're not going to take that book with you on your honeymoon!"

Nat promised he wouldn't even think about the book.

They honeymooned in Danvers. Nat saw again the little house with two rooms where he had lived. One evening they walked at twilight and scuffed autumn leaves. The new moon rose. Nat remembered the night, so long ago, when he had waited for Hab to go to sleep so he could work his good-luck spell.

If I still believed in spells . . . he thought.

Polly paused and looked up at the moon. "Give me some silver to jingle, Nat. Not that the book will need a good-luck spell." She jingled the silver solemnly. For a moment she was silent. "Nat, why don't we take the rest of our honeymoon after the book comes out?"

"Polly! You don't mean you want to go back to Salem now, and have me start working on the book?"

"That's exactly what I mean! Maybe you can forget about it, but I can't!"

Soon Nat was at work again — longer hours than ever. One night, when they had planned to go to a party, Nat looked up, all at once, remembering. It was midnight. He dashed to their bedroom. Polly was reading. He was so ashamed of himself that he snapped at Polly.

"The party! Why didn't you remind me?"

Polly looked unconcerned. "You know, I had the most awful headache."

Nat snorted. "You never had a headache in your life!"

"I know. That's why this one was so awful."

"You're fibbing and you know it!"

Polly grinned. "You can't prove a thing."

Nat began laughing.

"I'm becoming a terrible creature," Polly said. "Sometimes when people come to call, I say you're asleep."

One day, though, she did interrupt him for callers. "It's Father and Captain Prince! They're all on fire about something! I can tell."

The "something" was the idea of investing — the three of them — in a sealing ship. "There's a fortune to be made in a sealer," Captain Ingersoll declared, "and there's not the risk that there is in whaling. None of that staying out two, three, and four years, either. You know where the rookeries of the seals are and you know the season they gather there. You go — you round up the the young bulls — drive them off to the killing grounds and bang them over the head. And that is that."

"Almost as much profit as there is in the pepper

trade," Captain Prince said. "And none of the danger. No Malay gangs climbing up your cable and ripping your . . . uh . . . well . . . knifing you with those wavy daggers."

Captain Ingersoll walked the floor and smiled. "We've got our eye on a trim little craft — the *John*. We can put up two thirds of what it will take to outfit her. How about it, Nat? Do you want to put up the other third?"

"Right!" They shook hands on it.

Polly and Nat were at the wharf when the *John* sailed. Nat thought back over the years — the shilling he'd invested in Tom Perry's expectations — the hundred and thirty-five dollars he had risked in his first venture on the *Henry*. He'd come along a bit since then — with one-third interest in a sealer. "Polly," he said, "you've married a capitalist!"

"And a navigator," she said.

Nat pretended to groan. "That's a hint to get back to work. Slave driver!"

In the spring Nat finished the book. Before he presented the manuscript to Mr. Blunt, he took it to the East India Marine Society of Salem. Those were the men to judge the book — sailing masters, every one of them — who'd doubled the Cape or the Horn. They were the men who had spread the name of Salem so far and wide that natives of some distant islands thought Salem was a country — near the United States — and probably bigger. Yes, they were the men to sit in judgment on the book.

It was May 6 when the committee met to consider the book. On May 10, there was still no word.

"What *are* they doing, Nat?" Polly asked.

"Reading it — I hope."

Two more days crawled by; then, on May 13, their judgment came. Polly read the page-long letter, bristling with words like *amplitude, parallax,* and *refraction.* "Why don't they just say it's wonderful?"

Nat smiled. "They say it's *the most correct and ample* book on navigation in existence. From the East India Marine Society, that's praise! It's worth a ten-gun salute from any other men. Tomorrow, the manuscript goes to Mr. Blunt."

Polly smiled. "Well, that's done!"

"It's just begun. Now I start proofreading."

"Won't Mr. Blunt do that?"

"No one will proofread that book but me!"

"How long will it take you? A month?"

Nat chuckled and shook his head. "Bless you, Polly, I'll be lucky if it only takes a year."

When Nat was not busy with checking on the book, he did have time to enjoy his friends in Salem. He had long talks with Dr. Holyoke. What an amazing man he was! In 1799 he had celebrated fifty years of practice in Salem, and he declared he felt he could keep on for fifty more.

One evening he visited with Nat and Polly, and the talk turned to astronomy and Cadiz. "Like to see that observatory again, Nat?" he asked.

"Yes, but I probably won't."

Polly said, "He's swallowed the anchor. He's a capitalist now."

Dr. Holyoke chuckled and then scowled when a knock

came on the door. "Might as well answer it for you, Polly. It'll be someone for me. A doctor never spends a whole evening without an interruption. He — "

But it was someone to see Nat — Zack Selby. Zack was out of breath with running; his pig eyes were gloating. He could not wait to tell his news. The *John* had been stove in. The crew had been rescued by another boat, and just brought back to Salem. "But you fellows lost your shirts," Zack gloated, "when the *John* went down!"

Dr. Holyoke's eyes blazed; he doubled his fists.

Polly squeezed Nat's hand. "You're sure all the men are safe? Thank God for that!"

Zack sidled to the door before he fired his parting shot. "Thanks to God, maybe. No thanks to *books!*" And he scuttled out.

CHAPTER 22

SCIENCE AND SUMATRA

Dr. Holyoke went with Nat to see the crew and get word of the *John*. There was no doubt about the loss. Polly was waiting for them when they returned. She knew what rankled in Nat's mind — beyond the loss and the disappointment.

"Don't think about what Zack Selby said, dear — about books. Who's Zack Selby?"

Dr. Holyoke sighed. "He speaks for a lot of men, Polly. I'm not saying there are many as mean-spirited as he is — thank heaven. But there are hundreds — thousands — who don't believe in 'book sailing.' You know, seafaring is a lot like medicine. On the one hand — superstition and old wives' tales; on the other hand — the scientist, trying to solve the puzzles and find the answers. And all through the ages men have believed the superstitions and doubted the scientist. Natural, I suppose. You believe what you grow up believing. It's hard to change.

"You can't remember, Polly, when we first started inoculating for smallpox." He shook his head. "Wonder to me I wasn't lynched. Inoculation was risky — but not as bad as the epidemics of smallpox. Then vaccination came along. It was safer, but people raised almost as much fuss.

"All my life, I've felt as though I made three steps forward with science, and got dragged back two steps by the ignorance and superstitions of mankind. And every time a doctor 'loses' a patient, no matter why, it gives science another setback."

"And every time a ship is lost," Nat added, "it gives scientific navigation a setback, too. Men blame the books. They've been right to blame them, sometimes. There have been errors in the books. And when you depend on a book and it has a mistake, you'd have been safer not depending on it."

"But your book isn't going to have mistakes!" Polly said. "When men depend on it — "

Nat didn't smile. "It will take a long time to convince them."

Dr. Holyoke nodded.

Polly protested, "But after what the East India Society said — "

Dr. Holyoke smiled wryly. "That ought to convince all America — but Salem. A prophet is without honor in his own country, you know."

"What if England accepts the book? That would convince even Salem, wouldn't it?"

Nat laughed, but shook his head. "You could never

convince an Englishman that anything out of America was better than something made in England."

"Never?" Polly asked.

"Not a chance!" Nat told her.

Late in March, Dr. Holyoke brought them a Newbury paper. "Listen to this!" He read:

> "To the honor of the scientific knowledge of Mr. Nathaniel Bowditch of Salem, Mass., we are informed that one copy of his *New American Practical Navigator* was sold in London to two nautical booksellers by Mr. Blunt of this town, for 200 guineas, and an edition of 6,000 copies is now in press. Moore's *Practical Navigator* has depreciated very much in that country, owing to the numerous errors which have been fatal to mariners."

Polly's eyes glowed. "There, Nat! Who said England would never accept an American book? I guess the world will believe you now!"

"Maybe," Nat said, "if I'd been a sailing master myself, in full command of a ship . . ."

He said no more. But early in the summer he came home with something on his mind. He had been asked to go as captain, supercargo, and part owner on a voyage to Sumatra and the pepper islands. "I had a long talk with Mr. Lawrence today," he told Polly. "He has his eye on a new vessel — the *Putnam* . . . Well, Polly?"

Polly caught her breath, then smiled. "Master and supercargo, both? Captain Bowditch, you'll be a busy man!"

Nat hugged her. "Bless you, Polly."

He soon found he was a busy man. Preparations for the voyage kept him running here, there, and everywhere. In August, he had to make a trip to Boston. "I'm sailing in Miller's sloop," he said. "Lots more pleasant than a stagecoach in August."

"It'll help you get your sea legs again," Polly said. "Have a good trip."

"I shan't be long," Nat promised. Miller promised, too, "I'll have him back in short order, Mrs. Bowditch!" And they made the trip down in good time. But the morning they were ready to leave Boston, they were becalmed.

Miller was disgusted. "Of all the infernal luck," he growled. "I promised your wife I'd have you back in short order. Now look at me! Becalmed!"

On a sudden impulse Nat said, "It suits me fine. Today is Commencement Day at Harvard. I've always intended to go."

Miller eyed him suspiciously. "You're not just saying that to make me feel good?"

"No," Nat told him, "I've always wanted to go."

But when he sat alone in the crowd, and watched the fresh-faced boys getting their degrees, he knew it had been a mistake to come. It only brought back a heartache that was better forgotten. Harvard . . . Harvard men . . . In spite of everything the buried memories rose up to nag him.

Again he was a boy of twelve, sitting at the breakfast table, filled with bubbling joy because he was going to go back to school — he thought. Again he saw the frown on his father's face, and the tired shadows under Mary's eyes. Again he saw the paper that had sealed his fate for nine years: *Nathaniel Bowditch — Indentured.*

From the platform President Willard's voice interrupted Nat's thoughts. He heard a name that sounded something like *Bowditch,* dressed up in Latin. Some relative? Nat wondered.

When the ceremonies had ended, Nat walked slowly out into the sun again. He'd been a fool to come. He straightened, and tried to throw off the depression. "Forget it!" he told himself.

Behind him someone called, "Nathaniel Bowditch!" He turned. The years had whitened the man's hair, but Nat recognized him — the Mr. Morris who had offered him a chance to tutor his children — if he could have been free to leave the chandlery.

Mr. Morris gripped his hand. "Congratulations, Mr. Bowditch!" He put his arm around a young man's shoulders. "My son, John." He said, "John, this is Mr. Bowditch — the man I was telling you about! The man who got a degree from Harvard without ever setting foot in a classroom!"

"What?" Nat said.

"Didn't you hear them award it this morning? *Nathaniel Bowditch, A.M.*"

"I — I — suppose I was thinking of something," Nat said. In a happy daze he listened while Mr. Morris talked. In a happy daze he smiled and answered the boy's questions. *Nathaniel Bowditch — Harvard man!*

That night when he turned in, he lay smiling into the darkness. This, he told himself, was the proudest day of his life.

He had been home in Salem a few days when the letter came from Harvard:

Cambridge, August 31, 1802

Sir,

I have the pleasure of informing you officially that on Commencement day, the 25th instant, the degree of Master of Arts was conferred on you. It gives me further pleasure to acquaint you that this degree was unanimously voted by the Corporation of the University, and unanimously confirmed by the Overseers. . . .

I am, sir,
with much esteem
your very humble servant
JOSEPH WILLARD
President of Harvard College
Nathaniel Bowditch, A.M.

Polly said, "Oh, Nat! If only we could paint that on the *Putnam!* CAPTAIN BOWDITCH, A.M., COMMANDING"

Nat chuckled and hugged her. Bless Polly. He hadn't thought anything could make him happier than he had been on the twenty-fifth. But Polly had a way of sharing things.

"Come along up to my study," he said. "I have papers to sort. Work goes so much faster when you're there, too."

They were working that night in his study when someone hammered on the front door. They heard a hoarse shout, "Ahoy the ship!"

Polly jumped to her feet. "Something's happened!"

"Someone's been splicing the main brace," Nat

guessed. "I'll quiet him." He raced down the stairs, but not before more hammering fairly shook the house.

"*Ahoy the ship!*"

"I'll ahoy *you*," Nat muttered and flung open the door. "Just what the . . . Lem! Lem Harvey! Come in, man! Come in!" And Nat was bellowing as loud as Lem. "Polly! Come down and see who's here!"

Lem crushed Nat's hand and pounded his back and bellowed with cheerful profanity, "I knew there was one man in Salem who wouldn't think I was a ghost."

Nat wiggled his fingers to see if they still worked. "You're flesh and blood, all right, and bone and muscle! Come in, man, and sit down!"

Lem was too excited to sit down. He grinned at Polly, and paced the floor as he told his story. "When the *Betsy* struck, and we launched the boats, I headed straight out from land."

Nat said, "Good man!"

"There was six of us, when we started." Lem stopped for a moment. "I guess if the storm had let up, so we could have told where we were . . . But for two days we didn't do anything but fight the sea and bail that boat. Then . . . fog." He stood a moment, his shoulders slumped, staring into the past. "Man, were you ever lost in a fog? That's when they started cracking up. The first one . . ."

Polly shuddered.

Lem glanced at her and then skipped. "Well, the upshot of it was that I was picked up by the *Julius*, bound for Sumatra. What a journey that was. Everything that could happen to one ship happened to the *Julius*. But when we got to Sumatra, we did all right. The captain really got himself a cargo of pepper. And I got this!" He whipped out a short dagger with an ivory handle and a wavy blade.

"What in the world?" Polly asked.

"It's a creese, ma'am. A Malay dagger. They got all sizes and shapes — long, short, wavy, straight. But this is the one that works fastest. I was on anchor watch when I sort of *felt* something behind me. Didn't hear a thing! The way those brown devils can — begging your pardon, ma'am — can swarm up the cable . . . Well, anyhow, *he* got it instead of *me,* and then *I* got it . . . if you understand what I mean. I grabbed it, and — "

Nat interrupted hastily. "You say the captain did all right in Sumatra? A good cargo of pepper?"

"Yes, sir!"

"Would you like to go to Sumatra again?"

Lem stared. "Me? No, sir! Once is enough! If you ask me, once is too often!"

"Because of the way they fight?" Polly asked.

Lem shrugged. "Oh, that? That's not the half of it. You see, ma'am — "

Nat interrupted quickly again. "I'd like to talk to you about the business end of it, Lem. How they — "

Lem shook his head. "I don't know much about that part of it. All I know is that the captain and his clerk went ashore every day there was trading to do. Rest of us — we stayed on board and kept our fingers crossed that they'd get back! You see — "

Again Nat tried to haul him around on another tack. "Uh — how was the scenery?"

Lem shrugged again. "Full of trees . . . with a betel-chewing Malay behind each one. Remember the first time we saw a fellow chewing betel? And when he spit, it looked like blood? Man, you'd think the fellow's throat was cut. But they don't generally go for the throat with these daggers. They rip right into — "

It was no use. Nat said, "I'm sorry you wouldn't like to make another trip to Sumatra, Lem. I'm leaving soon for there, myself. Commanding the *Putnam*."

A grin split Lem's face. "You? Why didn't you say so? If you're going, I go, too! I'll sign on as anything from second mate to cook!"

Polly looked at him, puzzled. "But you said — "

Lem's gesture tossed it aside. "Aw, that was just *talk*. I was just — just — spinning yarns. Sumatra's fine. Pretty country. Real pretty."

"And the people?" Polly asked.

Lem scratched his head. "Uh — the people?" He looked at the dagger in his hand. "Uh — I'll bet they're nice, too, ma'am, when a fellow gets to know them. Now take this fellow that — uh — that I got the creese from. Probably wasn't anything *personal* about it. He didn't really have anything against me. It was just — just — " For a moment he was stumped, then he grinned. "Maybe he just run amuck! You know, they do that. All at once, they just get tired of living, and they go crazy. They start out with a whoop and a holler, knifing left and right, till someone . . ." He stopped again. "Look here, I'm keeping you folks up too late." He ambled to the door. "Remember, Captain Bowditch, I'm signing on the *Putnam*! Yes, sir! Now I'll clear for home, so you

can get some sleep!" He grinned at them, saluted —
with his dagger — and was gone.

Polly shuddered and hid her face in her hands. *"So
we can get some sleep* . . . he says! Oh, Nat!"

"Now, you mustn't mind the things Lem said. All
sailors — "

"It wasn't what he said," Polly told him. "It was what
he skipped. But I'm glad he wants to go with you."

"Yes," Nat agreed. "He's a master hand with the guns,
and when — I mean, he's an all-round — "

"Nathaniel Bowditch!" Polly was stern. "Don't you
start skipping things, too!"

Nat promised.

In November, a week before the *Putnam* was to sail,
a boy stopped with a message for Nat. "Dr. Holyoke says
to tell you he has it ready, sir."

Polly looked worried. "Is something wrong, Nat?"

"No, no! Just some supplies for the *Putnam.* Come
along with me."

Dr. Holyoke was waiting for them. Polly smiled at
him. "Dr. Holyoke, you're amazing; you could pass for
fifty!"

Dr. Holyoke said, "Bosh!" But he grinned. "Thing
that keeps me fit is keeping busy. I'll probably die with
my boots on. Doctors and sailing masters . . . Humph.
Well, here it is, Nat." He opened a small wooden chest.
"Some of everything you might need."

Polly gasped. "All that medicine? Is Nat sick?"

"No, no, child." Dr. Holyoke chuckled. "It's for his
crew. When a ship's off soundings, the captain's on his
own. 'Doctor, lawyer, merchant, chief.' " He looked
down into the chest. His eyes twinkled. "Plenty of jalap

there, Nat. Best thing in the world — if a man tries to soldier on you and play sick. Good dose of jalap. Don't think you'll have any trouble, though. Good men. I don't know about old Chad's grandson, Corey. Little skittery yet. Not enough keel there, or something. He'll probably work out, though."

Polly said, "Nat's depending a lot on Lem. I understand Lem's a good man with the guns."

Dr. Holyoke nodded. "Yes, and when you're in Sumatra . . . Humph. Now, let me see? Anything I forgot? Jalap, Peruvian bark, and — "

The door opened and Amanda Harvey stumbled into the room, panting. She needed the doctor right away. Lem had broken his leg.

CHAPTER 23

CAPTAIN BOWDITCH COMMANDING

"Come along with me, Nat," Dr. Holyoke suggested. "You might as well help set a leg. Six months from now, you might be bossing the job."

When they turned in at Lem's gate, they could hear him raging. When Lem saw them, he broke out afresh. He'd been mending the shingled roof of their little house when the ladder had slipped sideways. He'd tangled with it as he'd fallen.

"Me!" he stormed. "Me fall off of a house! Me that's hung by my eyebrows, reefing sail in a storm! Fix me up good, Doc, so I can be ready when the *Putnam* sails."

"Not a chance of it, Lem. This is a compound fracture."

"Now, listen, Doc —"

"Shut up, man! You'd be a nuisance on shipboard!"

"Oh . . ." Lem was silent. "Then, listen, Captain Bowditch. There's a lot I'd better tell you. When you hit the coral reefs off Sumatra . . ." Lem never stopped talking while the leg was set. Nat was glad Polly wasn't there to hear everything he said of Sumatra.

November 21 the *Putnam* sailed, "bound for Sumatra and the pepper islands, God willing" — Captain Bowditch commanding.

Captain Bowditch commanding. Nat looked about his ship and whispered those words to himself. He took his departure from Cape Ann. In his cabin, he marked his chart and started the log of the *Putnam*.

Billy Partel, his cabin boy entered. "Mr. Denny's compliments, sir. The watches are set."

Nat went on deck. Lupe's smile flashed, and was reefed. *Mr. Sanchez* now, second mate of the *Putnam*. A good man. A good crew, Nat thought. Old Chad Jensen at the wheel. Chad's grandson, young Corey, looked edgy. Probably hadn't found his sea legs yet. Good stuff in the boy.

Nat spoke to them quietly. He had good men in charge, he told them — Mr. Denny and Mr. Sanchez. They were to be obeyed at all times. He saw a flicker of bewilderment in the eyes of the crew. I suppose I should have roared, he told himself, but I can't think of anything to roar about. He told Mr. Denny and Mr. Sanchez he'd see them below at one bell.

When he talked to his mates he told them again — they were in charge. "Unless you need me, of course. But I don't expect you will."

They said, "Aye, aye, sir!" They went above.

Then for the first time the awful aloneness hit him. He was responsible — finally and completely. All the long, lonely way to the Cape, all the treacherous, squally weeks in the Indian Ocean — he was responsible. No matter what came up, night or day, if it baffled his men, he must decide.

For the first time he began to understand Captain Prince — the set of his jaw and the bite of his words when a voyage began — the eternal alertness that never relaxed. He knew now why Prince always seemed to shed about ten years when they made their landfall.

He thought of his father, his sloop aground on Anguilla Reef. He imagined how it must have been to watch, helpless, while his future was beaten to pieces. He remembered how Granny had said, "It took the tuck out of him."

He remembered the threat of battle off Cadiz, when he had pulled off his shoes and had gone to the powder room. He had forgotten where he was — had worked problems on a powder keg. He couldn't forget now. If battle threatened, he couldn't let others make the decisions.

If they were challenged now, he must decide — if he'd surrender his ship — if his men would die defending it. If he lost a man, he must answer the faces on the wharf when he returned: Lupe's young bride — Denny's wife and the two boys . . .

Nat shook his head and went topside. He'd have to stop that way of thinking. Not twelve hours from home. He'd be gone twelve months — maybe longer. He was sailing to an uncharted coast, in an untried ship. No man knew yet how the *Putnam* would sail.

In the days that followed, the *Putnam* proved herself with flying colors. She passed the *Eliza*, that had sailed six days before the *Putnam* weighed anchor. The crew of the *Putnam* shouted and swaggered. A good omen that! They'd set a record!

In February, they stood off Capetown to fill their water casks and replenish supplies. Then the last familiar landmark faded astern. With luck, their next landfall would be Sumatra. Thousands of miles yet to go. The Cape seemed next door to the East Indies — till a man had sailed the Indian Ocean.

Ten days from the Cape, Billy came to Nat with wide eyes. "Mr. Denny's compliments, s-s-sir. Could you come on deck? All — all — well *something's* broken loose!"

Nat checked the glass. It was falling. He went topside.

Mr. Denny said, "Craziest thing I've ever seen, sir. Hardly enough wind to make sternway, and the waves are pounding us to pieces."

Nat studied the sky; huge cumulus clouds. Another wave crashed on the deck. "A typhoon, Mr. Denny. The waves always outrun the wind. When the wind rises, we'll be able to make headway. We'll carry sail as long as possible. May outrun the storm."

Billy whispered, "How can we, sir? Typhoons move a hundred miles an hour, don't they?"

"They just go around that fast," Nat told him. "They don't move across the ocean at anything like that speed. You know how it is when you spin a top? It goes around very fast, and gradually moves across the floor?"

"Aye, aye, sir, I know about a top."

"Well, a typhoon — they call it a hurricane in the Caribbean — is just like a spinning wind-top. A huge top. It may be ten miles across — maybe twenty miles —

maybe bigger. The air may be whirling around a hundred miles an hour. But the wind-top moves across the ocean rather slowly — maybe only eight or ten miles an hour. So it is possible to outrun one."

"And — and — if we can't, sir? What then?" Billy's eyes were huge in his pale face.

"You heave to on a port tack — below the equator," Nat told him. "I'll tell you all about it some time, if you'd like to know."

"Yes, sir . . . I mean — Aye, aye, sir. I'd like that fine."

The hours passed. Eight bells; the watch was relieved; eight bells again, and the starboard watch lay below. The clouds were strange shapes now and tinged with copper; the wind freshened.

"Mr. Denny, have a lifeline rigged," Nat ordered.

"Aye, aye, sir."

Men stretched a heavy line the length of the *Putnam* from bow to stern. More wind; the tophamper creaked. Lupe grinned and shouted, "Long as she creaks she holds, eh?"

The rain began — a thin, driving mist. Eight bells again. But no one lay below now. It was all hands on deck.

More wind. When Nat finally gave the order to reef sail, the men lay aloft on the double.

Huge waves crashed over the *Putnam*. The rain poured until men ducked their heads in a crooked elbow to breathe. Two men at the helm now. The *Putnam* rolled, scuppers under.

Lupe staggered to keep his footing and shouted in Nat's ear, "Got the worst of it now, eh?"

Nat didn't try to answer. He knew this was just the beginning. If they were sucked into the center of the whirling wind-top there wasn't a ghost of a chance.

At last the wind lessened. The glass began to rise. The huge waves still pounded them, the torrents of water still poured down, but the worst was over. The typhoon was passing them.

It was two days later before the skies cleared and Nat could check their position and set his course once more for Sumatra. In early May they sighted the loom of shadowy mountains off their starboard bow.

When they reached the latitude of Susu Bay, they stood off until the sun was behind them. Then Nat sent a man to the foremast to watch for the coral reefs, and two men to the chains to sound. Warily they inched their way through coral reefs to their anchorage.

Other Salem captains were there, loading pepper. They asked news of home. Nat told them "news" — as of last November — and asked about pepper. They shook their heads. Not much chance for another ship to load at Susu. Not for weeks.

Nat weighed anchor, beat his way out through the treacherous coral, to Pulu Coya. More Salem captains there. They, too, asked news of home. They, too, shook their heads over the prospects of another ship loading pepper. Not for many weeks, they said.

At last the *Putnam* anchored at Tully Pas. More men wanting word from home; more men shaking their heads over the prospects of pepper. Maybe — when all the ships in port were loaded — maybe he could get pepper.

Nat waited. He waited through days and nights of heat

that seemed to come from an oven. The decks of the *Putnam* oozed tar.

Every day he went ashore to the village. All around him the squat brown men of Sumatra spoke politely — and each carried a creese in the folds of his sarong. Their ruler, the dato, was very polite. The captains, he said, were paying ten dollars for a picul of pepper. Perhaps if the captain of the *Putnam* would pay eleven? Nat said he'd wait.

More days passed. The heat bore down. The fragrance of frangipani, honeysuckle, and jasmine grew heavy enough to strangle a man. Nat longed for the tang of a sea breeze off the North Atlantic.

The dato was more polite. Pepper was coming in more and more slowly, he said. He feared the crop was running low. Perhaps if the captain of the *Putnam* could advance a small sum — say a thousand or so silver dollars? Then the dato could urge his men to greater effort. Nat said he'd wait. The dato sighed . . . and fingered his creese.

That night Nat could not sleep. He went topside to pace the deck. Somewhere he heard a snore. He went forward. Corey, who was on watch, was sleeping. Nat spoke quietly. "Corey . . . *Corey!*"

His voice brought old Chad running up the hatchway. "What's wrong, Captain? Is he hurt?" Chad's voice cracked. "Is he dead?"

Corey started and mumbled. "What? Aye, aye, sir!"

Chad roared, "You! Asleep on your watch!" The tongue-lashing he gave his grandson brought the whole crew topside.

What was it, they asked. Had the Malays tried to board?

"If they had," Nat roared, "you'd all be dead in your sleep!" He turned on his heel and went aft. There was nothing he needed to say to Corey. There was nothing he could say to the heartbroken old man who was Corey's grandfather.

More days crawled by. At last the dato said he would have pepper for the *Putnam* tomorrow.

The next morning Nat gave Mr. Denny orders: he was to begin unloading ballast so he could store pepper. He was not, under any condition, to let more than two Malays on board ship at one time.

Nat took Lupe ashore with him. The boat crew landed the scales and a money chest, and carried them to the square. The boat returned to the *Putnam*. Lupe and Nat were alone, in a swarm of bandy-legged, barrel-chested, powerful brown men. More and more men swarmed into the square with their baskets of pepper to be weighed and stored in bags.

Finally the pepper bags made a wall, shoulder high. If the captain would pay now, the dato said, the men would begin taking the pepper to the ship. The price was . . . twelve dollars per picul.

Nat did not hesitate. He slammed down the lid on the money chest. "Mr. Sanchez, call a boat for us. We'll get pepper somewhere else."

Lupe's smile stretched; his eyes were flat black and watchful. He prowled from the square and left Nat alone in the swarm of Malays. Two minutes passed, three . . . and five. More brown men thronged into the square. A violent argument rose. Nat wished he had had a grammar and dictionary of their language, too. It might have helped — to know what they were saying.

At last the dato approached him, smiling, his hand on his creese. It had been very hard work, he said, but he had persuaded the men to give up their pepper at eleven dollars a picul. The men were sad. It was choice pepper — the best of the season. That much was true, Nat knew. When the pepper began ripening in January, it ripened on the lower branches first. Not until May were the men harvesting the best of the crop.

Eleven dollars a picul? Nat opened the money chest again. When Lupe returned, the Malays were shouldering the pepper bags, and hurrying to the water's edge, loading their proas.

Lupe smiled again and this time the grin reached his eyes. "Señor," he drawled, "you are quite a guy."

Nat and Lupe went to the beach and watched the boats speed toward the *Putnam* — ten boats — more than fifty men. As they watched, a ladder dangled from the *Putnam*. Instantly a dozen Malays were laying hold, ready to climb. They could hear the angry shouts. Then they saw Denny, Watson, and Jensen appear at the rail — with muskets. The Malays edged back. Two went on board.

Nat and Lupe returned to the square to buy more pepper. The next day the dato was sad. Why couldn't his men help on the *Putnam?* They could save the white men much work at stowing the cargo.

Lupe explained. With his mirthless smile and his watching eyes, he explained. Their captain, he said, was a harsh man. He liked to work his crew hard. "Also," he murmured to Nat, "we do our own work — we live longer, eh?"

June passed, and half of July. More ships anchored at Tully Pas. One morning when Nat went ashore, the dato spread his hands and sighed. The two hundred piculs he had promised for today — it would be impossible to get.

"I wonder," Lupe muttered, "how much who is paying for pepper? Now what? Do we — wait him out again?"

Nat smiled. "No — we don't wait him out. We sail. We'll complete our cargo with coffee at the Isle of Bourbon or the Isle of France." He told Lupe of the two French islands east of Madagascar in the Indian Ocean. "I made my first sea voyage to Bourbon," he said. How long ago it seemed!

When they reached the Isle of France, three ships of Salem and Beverly were there. Polly's father, Captain Ingersoll, was just ready to weigh anchor. He came aboard the *Putnam* to see Nat and get news to take home to Polly. "How was it in Sumatra? Any trouble?"

"Oh, no," Nat told him, "quite uneventful."

Lupe's grin spread. "Captain Bowditch, he is one guy."

Captain Ingersoll cocked his head to one side. "So nothing happened, eh? I see . . . Well, I'll tell Polly all is well, and to look for you soon after I arrive. It shouldn't take you more than a week to load coffee here."

They cheered Captain Ingersoll on his way.

Nat said, "Mr. Denny, call the men aft."

Soon his men stood facing their captain — a tired crew, haggard with the long months of heat and the grinding toil of the passage to the Isle of France. He knew that every man standing there wanted at least a week on shore before they sailed. He said, "Captain Ingersoll tells me there's plenty of coffee to complete our cargo. Then — when we've wooded, watered, and provisioned, we'll weigh anchor. And we won't wet that anchor again till Salem Harbor. Do we — bear a hand?"

They split the air with cheers. In five days the *Putnam* stood out from the island.

When Nat had taken his departure, he did some figuring. It had taken the *Henry* eleven weeks from Bourbon to Salem. The *Putnam* was faster. With luck, they'd be home in early November — maybe even the last of October.

They ran into a storm that night. For days they lived in wet clothes and ate cold food. The *Putnam* was rolling much too heavily for the cook to make fire in the galley. They doubled the Cape and fought head winds. No speed from the *Putnam* now; she seemed to crawl. With a fair wind abaft the beam, the ship could have logged a hundred and fifty miles in a day's sailing. Now she fought head winds from tack to tack, and some day's sailing did not take her fifteen miles nearer home.

"When the storms are over," Lupe said, "we make up for it, eh?"

But the storms were never over. For several days at a time Nat was not able to take a sight. October passed; November came. With luck, Nat told himself now, they'd be home by early December. With good luck, he added.

In December they reached the Roaring Forties of the North Atlantic and groped their way, close hauled, in the teeth of the gales. At last the storms subsided.

At six bells of a forenoon watch, Nat said, "Mr. Denny, heave to for soundings."

Watson carried the deep-sea lead forward, and the other men followed, each with fakes of the line coiled in his hand — Collins on the cathead, Sandy in the fore chains, and Jensen in the main chains. Mr. Denny was on the quarter-deck with the rest of the line coiled.

Denny sang out, "All ready there, forward?"

Watson bellowed, "Aye, aye, sir!"

"Heave!"

"Watch, ho, watch!" It was Collins on the cathead. "Watch, ho, watch!" From Sandy in the fore chains. "Watch, ho, watch!" It was Jensen in the main chains.

Mr. Denny sang out, "Sixty fathoms!"

They hauled in the lead. Nat checked it. Black mud! They were off Block Island.

"Block Island!" Lupe grinned. "Next door to home — and the storm is dying!" But the storm raged again, as though it had been gathering its strength for one more assault on the *Putnam*. Long days passed. The fifteenth of December, when they sounded, the lead brought up sand.

"Off Nantucket!" Lupe said. "I dress in my go-ashore clothes!" Then the stormy North Atlantic proved that all the other gales had been mere child's play. For seven days and nights the *Putnam* was deluged and hammered.

At last the skies cleared. Nat made his observations. "I could have swum from Nantucket that fast!" he muttered.

Clouds darkened the sky again. For three days the rain poured in the waterfall torrents of tropical storms.

Only this rain was cold, and mixed with sleet. And men struggled with numb fingers to reef and loose sails.

In his cabin, Nat rested his head on his hands. He had hoped to be home in early November — with luck the end of October. Christmas Eve — and they weren't home yet.

Something clawed at his attention. He looked around, puzzled, then realized what it was. The wild rolling and pitching of the *Putnam* had lessened. At eight bells, Mr. Denny came to his cabin.

"The rain's letting up?" Nat asked.

"Aye, aye, sir." Mr. Denny was grim. "This is worse."

"Worse?"

"Yes, sir. Fog." He shook his head slowly from side to side. "I've seen fogs in my day, but this one . . . " He shrugged, and his shrug was a shiver. *"Fog!"*

CHAPTER 24

MAN AGAINST THE FOG

Morning came, but no sunlight. The only way a man could know that day had come was because the fog turned pale. From amidship, a man could not see the bow; he could not even see the foremast. The lookouts strained to see what lay before them, and shook their heads in despair. "If anything's there," one muttered, "we'll find it when we hit it!"

Eight bells came; the starboard watch lay below. In the fo'c'sle the men huddled and slewed sidelong glances at each other. When they spoke they growled in low voices, as though the fog that shrouded the world had muffled their words.

Jensen came below from his trick at the wheel. "You know what the Old Man said to me?" The men looked up without speaking, without moving their heads. "He came alongside me and stood there, watching the compass. He said, 'You have a steady hand on the wheel, Chad; your wake is straight as a string.' "

Corey's voice rose and cracked. "How does he know? Can't see our wake, can we? Can't see anything!"

Jensen nodded. "That's what I said to him. I said, 'Maybe, sir, if we could see it.' Know what he said to me? He said, 'We don't have to see it to know that, do we, Jensen? We just watch the compass and know. Simple matter of mathematics, isn't it?' And he went below again, cool as you please."

Corey shook his head, as a dog shakes when he comes out of water. "Three days with no sun, no moon, no stars to tell us where we are."

Jensen stopped smiling. "Getting thicker, too." He shook his head. "I'd as soon play blindman's bluff on a cliff as sail through this fog."

Watson stared at the deck. "All right, maybe, if we had sea room. But what do we know about where we are now?"

Corey slumped forward, his elbows on his knees, his hands dangling. "Three days of zigging and zagging. Makes your muscles pull, just thinking about it — how many times we've hauled around on another tack. Zig and zag . . . zig and zag . . . how can a body expect to know where we are?"

Jensen grinned wryly. "We've had plenty practice — most the way home. Ought to be used to it, maybe."

Corey's voice cracked again. "We had sea room then. Sea room! But we were off Nantucket Shoals ten days ago! *Where are we now?*"

Jensen gripped Corey's shoulder. "Easy, lad. Maybe the fog will lift."

But the fog did not lift. Eight bells bong-bonged and it was noon. The fog grew thicker. All around was a ghost world now. From forward, ghost voices of the leadsmen chanted the soundings. From aft, ghost voices spoke as men heaved the log and turned the glass.

The wind freshened and blew in fitful gusts. Jensen said, "Good! It'll blow the fog away!"

It did not. It only blew more clouds of fog to roil and billow over the *Putnam*.

Along about three bells Nat came on deck with his spyglass and went to the larboard rail. The word passed swiftly. "Something's up! The Old Man's taking charge!"

Mr. Denny stood at Nat's shoulder. "Impossible to see anything, isn't it, sir?"

Nat answered without turning. "If the fog lifts one half minute, we can see it."

Mr. Denny stared into the fog, too. The minutes crawled by; the ghost bell marked the leaden-footed time: *bong-bong, bong-bong.* Mr. Denny shifted his feet and sighed. Nat was motionless. His glass never wavered from the point toward which he stared. The brief day began to darken. Eight bells again; the starboard watch was relieved.

Watson said, "The Old Man's watching for something. S'pose it's the light on Baker's Island?"

Corey shouted, "Baker's Island! Are you crazy? Think we'd get close enough to Baker's Island to see the light in this fog? And fetch up on the rocks somewhere? You crazy fool! Ever seen a ship on Gales Ledge? Or Whale-back? Baker's Island light? You crazy fool!"

Jensen gripped Corey's shoulder again. "Easy, lad. We got sea room. Ain't anywhere near Baker's Island."

Through the white ghost world they heard Nat's voice. "That's it, Mr. Denny! Baker's Island! We're exactly on our course!"

Jensen gasped. Corey whimpered and muttered a prayer. Jensen said, "We'll anchor now, lad. We'll stand off till the fog lifts."

Nat's voice spoke again through the fog. "Two men in the chains, Mr. Denny, and keep heaving those leads!" He moved briskly to the side of the helmsman. "West northwest by west."

"Aye, aye, sir. West northwest by west it is, sir."

Night came again. Darkness and fog shrouded the *Putnam*. Nat stood near the compass, holding his watch so that he could read the face in the glow of the binnacle lamp.

Watson in the larboard chains sang out, "By the deep ten."

From the starboard chains Kedzie yelled, "And a quarter less four!"

The helmsman stared at the compass; his knuckles whitened on the wheel.

Somewhere in the mist Corey gasped, "It's shoaling!"

Nat's gaze never left his watch. He lifted one finger, as though with one finger he could control the wind and the waves that hurled a ship, a crew, and three hundred tons of cargo toward the waiting rocks. "Now! Due west!"

"Due west it is, sir."

The minutes crawled. The ship's bell bong-bonged.
Kedzie rumbled, "By the deep six."

In the foggy darkness someone tried to laugh, and it
sounded like a sob.

Watson sang out, "And a half less six!"

Nat stared at his watch, and he lifted his finger again.
Kedzie yelled, "By the deep four!"

Nat said, "West by north."

The helmsmen swung the wheel hard, growled at himself, and steadied on the course. "West by north it is,
sir."

No sound but the ship's bell now.

Watson's singsong came through the darkness. "By the
mark five."

And Kedzie's rumble answered, "By the mark five."

Jensen said, "The Old Man goes ahead like it was
noonday! He — "

Watson's singsong again. "And a half less five."

Kedzie's rumble answered. "And a half less five."

Watson's voice sharpened. "And a quarter less three!"

Nat gave no sign that he heard. He stared at his watch.

Kedzie's voice again. "And a quarter less three!"

Nat said, "Steady as you go."

Watson yelled, "And a half less three!"

Somewhere in the fog Corey screamed, "It's shoaling,
I tell you! We're going aground! We'll be beaten to
pieces!"

Nat did not raise his eyes. He hardly lifted his voice
to say, "Mr. Sanchez, it would be a kindness if Corey
could sleep."

Lem Harvey and Polly Bowditch

Lupe purred, "Aye, aye, sir." In the darkness a fist thudded; a body hit the deck; a slurring scrape said someone was dragging the sleeping Corey forward.

Nat lifted his finger again. "Southwest by south."

In the big white house facing the Common, the tall clock struck nine. Polly rose from her place by the fire, went to the window, shaded her eyes from the light, and stared out into the mist.

Lem Harvey looked up and shook his head. "It's no use, Mrs. Bowditch, ma'am. Won't be any ships make port tonight."

Polly sighed and turned from the window. "I know. But I did so hope he'd be home by Christmas Day."

"Better pray now he don't come."

Polly gasped, "Lem! What do you mean?"

"Nothing, ma'am. Just that the only sailor that'd turn up in Salem tonight would come by land. Because he'd been wrecked somewhere and put ashore."

"Lem, what's happened? What are you keeping from me?"

"Nothing, ma'am."

"There is something," she insisted. "That's why you came tonight. What's happened, Lem?"

His black eyes met Polly's gaze squarely. "I swear, ma'am, it's nothing like that. I just came because — well — I got to thinking about you. I knew the folks was away and you were alone in the house. I just got to thinking about you alone on Christmas night, ma'am. That's all. It's the only reason. I swear it is. You believe me, don't you, ma'am?"

"Yes, Lem, I believe you." For a few minutes she sat

by the fire, staring into the glow. Then she was at the window again, staring into the blank wall of fog.

Lem said, "Honest, Mrs. Bowditch . . . "

Polly turned from the window. "I know. You're right, Lem. Of course you're right." She started back to her chair, stopped, whirled, and stood motionless, listening. "I could swear I heard Lupe call out!"

"If you did, ma'am, it was his ghost."

This time Polly clutched his arm and shook it. "Lem! What is it! You've got to tell me!"

Lem stood. "Nothing, ma'am. Only that the *Putnam* ain't coming in. I mean — she ain't coming *tonight!* You got sense enough to know that, ma'am. There's some things a master just don't do. And bringing his ship into Salem Harbor in a fog like this is one! I tell you . . . Where are you going, ma'am?"

Polly didn't answer. She hurried into the hall, flung the big door wide, and stood there, staring into the fog.

From the fog Nat's voice called, "Polly! Is that you?"

"Nat! Oh, Nat, darling!"

He raced up the steps and had her in his arms. "Oh, Polly, it's so good to be home!" After a little he chuckled. "Good thing you opened the door, though. The fog's so thick I might have gone right past the house!" Still chuckling, his arm around Polly, he closed the door and went in by the fire. "Why, Lem! How good to see you!"

At first Lem didn't answer, he only stared, his jaw sagging. "It's really you! What happened? Where's the *Putnam?*"

Nat tossed off his jacket. "Right down in Salem Harbor, riding to anchor." He stood by the fire, rubbing his hands. "Why?"

"You came in through this fog?"

Polly said, "When it's so thick you almost missed the house?"

Nat shrugged. "Oh, that's different. On the *Putnam* I had log, lead and lookout." He grinned. "Not that the lookout's been seeing much."

Lem growled, "When did you last shoot the sun?"

"About three days ago."

Lem gulped. "Three days? Seventy-two hours? And since then?"

"It's simple mathematics, Lem. At such a speed, in so many hours, you log so many miles in a given direction. It's — "

"Yeah," Lem growled. "Seventy-two hours through the Roaring Forties. Seventy-two hours by dead reckoning, and then you enter Salem Harbor. Why, you . . . begging your pardon, ma'am, for what I'm thinking." He slumped in a chair and stared at Nat.

Nat winked at Polly. "Have you any idea what's the matter with him?"

Polly's eyes danced. "He just doesn't understand about you and mathematics, dear. Two plus two is four. It comes out right, doesn't it?"

Lem shifted in his chair and growled under his breath. Hurrying footsteps thudded on the porch. A heavy fist hammered on the door. Polly went to open it. Zack Selby entered, panting, talking as he came. "I'm sorry about the bad news, ma'am! Someone said they saw him on the street! I'm sorry he lost the *Putnam,* ma'am. He — "

Lem roared, "Come in and stop bellowing, you fool! The *Putnam's* riding at anchor in Salem Harbor!"

Zack stared at Nat. "You — you — come in through the fog? How'd you do it?"

Lem threw back his shoulders and bellowed, "How'd you think he did it? Book sailing! Simple matter of mathematics!" He picked up his jacket and cap. "I'd better explain things to folks, or you two won't get any rest tonight! Come along, Zack!" The door slammed.

Polly's lips quirked. "Lem's going to have a wonderful time." She looked at Nat with glowing eyes. "It's really you! Captain Bowditch, F.A.A. and A.M., I'm very proud of you!" She blinked back sudden tears. *"Oh, Nat, it's been so long!"*

Nat's arm tightened around her. Somewhere out of the past a voice whispered, *"A long time to sail by ash breeze."*

"Was it awfully hard?" Polly asked.

"Not too bad," Nat told her. "Rough weather sometimes. But I'll say this for it — I was never becalmed!"